Bigfoot]

Idaho

Mysterious Encounters

Frank Hendersen

Table of Contents

Introduction

For centuries, tales of ape-like creatures have been told around campfires and in dark corners. But in the bustling state of Idaho, stories of ape-like sightings are more than just tall tales; they are evidence that Bigfoot exists.

Bigfoot in Idaho: Mysterious Encounters is a compilation of stories from eye-witnesses who have seen the ape like creature roaming the idyllic landscape of our beloved state. From a young girl on her fourwheeler to an avid hiker who stumbled upon one unexpectedly, these accounts prove with vivid detail that something extraordinary lies beyond what we can see.

Each story captures a unique experience that has left its mark on those who witnessed it firsthand. These stories will draw you in and make you question everything you know about the natural world. You'll feel a thrill as you read of these remarkable encounters and imagine what it would be like to have your own.

So, if you're looking for something extraordinary, this book is an absolute must-read! Each story serves as an invitation to explore our state with fresh eyes; each one giving us more insight into the mysterious ape-like creature that has become so prevalent in Idaho's forests and trails.

But don't just take our word for it - go out there yourself and search for Bigfoot! Who knows, maybe you'll be the lucky one who finds him hiding away deep in those woods. Read through this incredible collection of stories and let your curiosity take you far beyond what's visible.

So, reader, come with us on this remarkable journey and discover the truth about Bigfoot in Idaho. With every page turned, you'll find yourself being drawn into the mysterious world of ape-like creatures that lies just beyond our vision. Let go of your fears and join us as we explore these incredible encounters - who knows where it might lead!

ENCOUNTER #1 Sun Valley Encounter

It was summer and my wife and I had been married for a few years. We were both interested in the mysterious ape-like creature known as Bigfoot, which many people thought to inhabit forests of the northwest United States. We'd heard stories from others about their sightings, but we wanted to experience one ourselves. That's why we decided to take a camping trip out to Sun Valley Idaho in search of this elusive creature.

My wife, Sarah, and I had been together for nearly five years. We were childhood sweethearts, having grown up in the same small town. Although we had wanted to start a family of our own one day, the timing just hadn't been right yet. In the meantime, we both worked hard at full-time jobs; she as an accountant and I as a software engineer. Our lives were comfortable and predictable but lacked something special that we couldn't quite put our fingers on - until one day when talk of Bigfoot began circulating through the small town grapevine.

We knew immediately this was the kind of adventure we'd been looking for! With no children to worry about yet, it was time to take a chance and set off on a camping trip in search of this creature. Sarah and I packed up our camping gear and headed out to Sun Valley Idaho, determined to have at least one big adventure before settling down into the daily routine of raising a family.

We arrived in the late afternoon and quickly set up camp beneath the tall pines trees that dotted the landscape. We had heard stories from other locals about strange noises coming from deep within the woods, so we decided to take an evening walk around our campsite - just in case we were lucky enough to catch a glimpse of Bigfoot! As we walked along, everything was peaceful and quiet until suddenly there was an eerie hooting sound echoing through the trees. We both looked at each other.

We listened for a few moments and soon realized it was nothing more than an owl. Disappointed, we continued our walk. The night was so moonlit that it was easy to make out the trails nearby our campsite. We ambled along in companionable silence, occasionally stopping to look up at the stars twinkling overhead. Despite being on high alert for any sign of Bigfoot, everything remained peaceful and still.

After what felt like hours of walking, we had made it back to our campsite without any other strange sounds. As we settled into bed, I couldn't help but feel a little bit disappointed that we hadn't seen anything; however, I reassured myself that our search was far from over yet! With one more day of camping ahead of us, I was determined to make the most of it and hopefully return home with a story that would leave our friends in awe. Little did I know, what we were about to experience would be far greater than anything we could have imagined!

I awoke early the next morning, and knew that Sarah was still fast asleep in our tent. I decided to surprise her by making a fire and cooking breakfast. As I went about gathering kindling for the fire, I paused to appreciate my luck being able to spend this time with my wife in such a beautiful setting. We had something special here – not only were we sharing an adventure together but also a common interest of searching for Bigfoot.

I soon had a nice blaze crackling away and set about preparing some eggs and bacon over it. As I cooked, I kept looking out into the wilderness, imagining what sorts of creatures could be lurking beyond our camp site. Would today finally be the day when we might get lucky enough to spot the ape-like creature we had heard so much about? My anxiety and anticipation for the day swelled within me as I finished up breakfast.

I set out a plate of food for Sarah and then woke her with a gentle shake. When she opened her eyes, Sarah was delighted to see that I had already cooked breakfast! After sharing a few moments of blissful appreciation of our surroundings, we ate and then set off in search of Bigfoot once again. This time, it felt like luck was on our side…

We set off up a trail, where there had reportedly been a Bigfoot encounter about four years ago. We hiked for an hour and a half, eager to reach the location that so many stories had been told about. When we arrived, it was surreal to be standing in the same spot where other people may have encountered the ape-like creature.

We looked around for any signs of Bigfoot, but our search yielded no results. We decided to take a break and enjoyed a snack under the shade of nearby trees before continuing on with our journey. This was already turning out to be a perfect morning, and as we sat there discussing our plans for today's search, we suddenly heard a distant thudding sound. It repeated about five times, and we stared at each other in awe. Could it really be Bigfoot? Our hearts raced with excitement as we quickly packed up and followed the sound into the forest.

We had a general idea of where sounds might be from, so we set off with eager anticipation. As we walked along the trail, we both kept our ears open for any sounds that could indicate an ape-like creature was nearby. Sure enough, after a few minutes of walking, we heard a distinct series of thuds in the distance again. We looked at each other with excitement; this is one of the classic signs of Bigfoot! With accelerated hope, we picked up our pace and followed the sound deeper into the woods. Who knew what surprises lay ahead? Our adventure was just beginning…

We continued our journey for another 45 minutes, and sure enough the distant thudding noise was heard again. This time it was much closer, sounding loud and distinct – like a powerful creature was hitting wood hard enough to make such a sound! We were filled with anticipation as we followed the mysterious knocks deep into the woods.

Scanning our surroundings eagerly, yet nothing seemed out of place. Still, the ape-like creature had to be close by – the knocks were getting louder with every passing minute. We kept walking further into the woods, our hearts racing with anticipation. As we rounded a bend, I suddenly caught sight of movement in the distance and pointed it out to Sarah. We both stopped dead in our tracks, hardly daring to breathe as we watched the ape-like figure slowly move away from us.

We had finally spotted Bigfoot! Our hearts raced with excitement as we watched the majestic creature before it disappeared back into the woods. We were filled with awe at such an incredible experience – our search for Bigfoot in Idaho had finally paid off! After watching until it was completely out of sight, we made our way slowly back to camp, feeling overwhelmed and euphoric.

We discussed that the ape-like creature must have stood at least 7 feet tall and was covered in dark fur. Its movements were graceful yet powerful as it moved through the brush and trees effortlessly. Even from that distance of about 200 yards, its presence was undeniable - there was no doubt in our minds that this ape-like figure was indeed Bigfoot. The view may have been brief, but it was remarkable and we were mesmerized by what we had just seen.

Afterwards, I wished that we'd taken some photos of the incredible moment but sadly the excitement had caught us off guard so completely that we forgot all about it. As night fell, we started a campfire to make dinner—pasta and steak that we had packed for a special last dinner out on our Bigfoot hunt. The meal was excellent and as we laid down for bed, we couldn't stop talking about the amazing experience.

Just as we began to doze off, we heard those strange knocks again - this time much further away and only a few times. Then it faded away into the night. We caught our breath in wonderment, knowing that it had been the ape-like creature that we'd seen earlier in the day. Instead of fear or trepidation, all we felt was an intense excitement at having encountered Bigfoot!

The next morning, filled with eagerness but without any more occurrences, we packed up and headed home. This special encounter made us long for another trip–we spent the following year returning to this place three more times and were better prepared each time with GoPro cameras always at-the-ready and sound recording devices. Yet, we never again heard anything that sounded like Bigfoot. We had truly been lucky on our first Bigfoot expedition and while we still hope to have another encounter, who knows if that will be our once-in-a-lifetime experience?

ENCOUNTER #2 A Paperboy's Enconter with Bigfoot

I had been delivering papers for two years now, and I was just finishing up my route on my bicycle as the autumn air filled with a crisp chill. I had started this job when I was only twelve because I wanted something to do and needed some extra cash of my own in order to buy a new video game; but after two years of paper-boying, I found that I truly enjoyed the freedom that it gave me - enough money to buy the video games and name brand clothes my parents thought were unnecessary.

As the fog rolled in, it created an air of mystery around me. The poor visibility was something I had grown accustomed to over my two-year stint as a paper boy. Despite the lack of clarity, I knew every twist and turn of these suburban roads like the back of my hand; my route was mostly made up of cookie cutter homes with ok sized yards. But there was one part of the route that went down a dead end and had homes on the right side of the road and an open field to my left. The mountains were in the distance, silhouetted by morning mist.

The lady that lived at the end of this road always left me such a big tip at Christmas because she knew her house was further away than the others. Little did she or I know that this year I would really earn that tip! As I made my way down this road with just five papers left, I could not help but notice something out in the field near the cattle that were grazing. There were a few hundred cattle out there, but one of them seemed out of the ordinary due to its size. However, because of the morning fog it was very difficult to make it out clearly. After finishing my route and delivering the last paper to the lady's house at the end of the road, I decided to take a closer look.

As I pedaled back down her driveway towards that open field ahead of me, my curiosity grew more intense. With each stroke of the pedal pushing me forward, my gaze shifted from the pavement to the side of the road in search for some sort of clue or answer. Initially, nothing seemed out of the ordinary in the vast expanse of land; however, as I kept looking over there where I had originally spotted something peculiar earlier, a wave of goosebumps broke upon my skin - there it was again!

I had stopped in my tracks and could not believe my eyes; there, standing less than 100 yards away, was an ape-like creature larger than any of the cattle. Despite the heavy fog I could now clearly make out its broad and strong build. It seemed to be surveying the movements of the animals in the field, oblivious to my presence.

The figure stood firmly on two legs with arms that went well past its knees. Its fur appeared matted and greyish-brown in coloration. As I observed this mysterious creature from afar, a wave of fear and awe came over me - what was it? A shiver ran down my spine as I realized that I was witnessing something truly extraordinary.

I stayed as still as a statue, not wanting to startle the creature and scare it away. After watching it for a few moments, the ape-like figure suddenly took off at an incredible speed towards the cattle. I was taken aback by its velocity; even though the herd of cows were attempting to flee, they could never match its pace. Its movements appeared flawless and swift - similar to an Olympic sprinter chasing down a five year old child - there was just no comparison in their speed.

My heart raced as I watched this once in a lifetime sight unfold before me. In that moment my mind became flooded with questions: what kind of creature was this? Was it native to Idaho? Where did it come from?

The ape-like figure suddenly jumped on one of the cows, and quickly broke its neck with its massive hands and muscular arms. Its fur was dark brown in color, and the cow was put out of its misery in just a moment, only making one loud bellow before dying. I had just witnessed this thing kill a large animal effortlessly.

I froze in shock, unable to tear my gaze away from the ape-like creature who had just killed a cow. The beast composed itself and picked up the cow with ease, even though the animal must have weighed at least 1,000 pounds. It effortlessly cradled it with two arms and headed towards the distant mountains.

The creature was moving slower now but still extremely fast considering it was carrying a dead cow. I watched as long as I could until it eventually faded into the morning fog that covered the distance between myself and where the mountains were located. In total, my sighting of this mysterious creature lasted about 10 minutes before it completely disappeared from view.

Afterwards, I continued to sit on my bike on the side of the road for a few minutes, still in awe and wonder. It was then that a lady drove out from her driveway in her car, clearly heading into town for some shopping. She noticed me sitting there and pulled up next to me, obviously curious as to what I was doing. When I told her about my sighting, she looked at me with shock - it seemed like she had heard stories about ape-like creatures before.

I proceeded to describe the creature in great detail; it was around eight feet tall with broad shoulders, a muscular build and greyish-brown fur. Its hands were huge and its fingers appeared almost ape-like; its legs were long and powerful, capable of running at incredible speeds. She listened intently as I recounted the events that had just taken place; it was clear that she knew what kind of creature I had seen.

When I finished my story, the woman looked around nervously. She seemed startled and a bit concerned; it was clear that she had knowledge of these ape-like creatures roaming around Idaho from time to time. Without hesitation, she offered me a ride back home so I could tell my parents about the experience once they returned from work. We loaded my bike in her trunk and made the 10 minute drive to my house.

Upon arriving at my home, I thanked the kind lady again for giving me a ride. Unlocking the door and stepping inside to an empty house, I looked back to make sure the woman had gone before closing it firmly behind me. With newfound knowledge about this mysterious ape-like creature, I spent a few minutes sitting on the couch trying to absorb and further process my experience.

I decided to go on the family computer and do some research, soon discovering that these sightings were not completely uncommon in Idaho - in fact, it was actually considered a hot spot to see them. My searches revealed what this ape-like creature was called: Bigfoot. After looking at some of the pictures online, I knew without doubt that is exactly what I had seen.

The more research I did, the more amazed and slightly fearful I became of what could be out there in the vast wilderness areas surrounding my home. Bigfoot sightings were reported all over Idaho, with some even occurring closer to town than I would have expected. It seemed that this ape-like creature was both real and living right in our backyard.

That day marked a turning point in my life - it opened up new possibilities and perspectives on nature, as well as instilling a sense of mystery and awe at the same time. Though no one else believed me when I told them about my sighting, I knew for sure what I had seen that morning - an ape-like creature roaming around Idaho's wild places. I would go on to read stories from other witnesses who had seen similar ape-like creatures, and it was comforting to know that I wasn't alone in my experience.

ENCOUNTER #3 Skiing in Idaho: Our Encounter with Bigfoot

The cold winter air filled our lungs as my wife and I loaded our skis for a day of skiing at Bogus Basin Ski Resort. We were determined to make the most of the break from school that our kids – 14 and 11 years old – had been granted, so we took this opportunity to continue the tradition of taking them skiing at least three times a year ever since they were four. The snow was fresh and inviting, begging us to take part in a perfect day together.

We packed up from our house in Boise at around 8am for the trip to Bogus Basin Ski Resort, stopping at the local Starbucks for some warm beverages for the drive. As kids tend to do, they spent most of the way there playing on their phones, but we still managed to mix in some conversation as well. We arrived at the resort with plenty of time before it opened and so we could take our time getting ready and preparing ourselves for a day of skiing ahead. The air was cold but filled with excitement and anticipation - we were all looking forward to this ski trip! We changed into our gear quickly and got onto the chairlift just in time, eager to get going.

The day flew by quickly, with laughter, joy and exhaustion in equal measure. We delighted in watching our kids as they became more daring and experienced as skiers, remembering the days when we had to help them just to get down a slope. At lunchtime, we decided to take a break from skiing and refuel at one of the restaurants onsite - it was nice to sit back and enjoy each other's company away from the cold air outside. After recharging our batteries, we spent the rest of the afternoon trying out different slopes that challenged us all - some were easier than others but none were too difficult. By 8:00pm, we had worked up quite an appetite so decided to head home for for a very late dinner.

We packed up our gear, taking in the sight of the mountains before leaving for the night. The kids were tired but excited to share their day's story with friends on social media, so they were completely focused on their phones in the back seat. As we drove down the windy roads away from the resort, my wife and I talked more about the day and started thinking about what we would do with the rest of the weekend. Suddenly my wife yelled out in surprise after seeing something standing off to the side of the road about 50 feet ahead.

We quickly looked and caught a quick glimpse of an ape-like creature standing there, half hidden by the darkness! We passed it by quickly, in disbelief as to what we had just seen. Both our kids looked up and asked what had happened; my wife and I quickly exchanged glances before she said "nothing". We continued to drive cautiously, silently replaying the image of the creature that we had just seen in our minds again and again. Despite being a little shaken from the experience, we eventually managed to get back home safely.

We all got out of the car and began unpacking our things for the night. I made sandwiches and fruit for us all so that we could have something to eat before putting the kids to bed. They were so excited from the day that their minds were racing, but in the back of my wife's and I's minds we were thinking about what we had seen. After ensuring the children were asleep, we started talking softly about our experience; discussing what it might have been.

We tried to describe as best as possible what exactly we saw - an ape-like creature, standing tall and strong with broad shoulders and muscular arms and legs. Its dark matted fur glinted slightly in the moonlight, giving it an almost mysterious appearance. It stared at us with a stoic expression, its eyes intense and focused despite the darkness that surrounded it. The ape-like creature easily stood 8 feet tall and seemed unafraid of our presence; something about it made us believe that this was not just any animal we had come across but something far more extraordinary. We were both left speechless by what we had seen - could this really be the mythical bigfoot of Idaho?

We couldn't believe what we had seen and eventually fell asleep after talking at length about this experience, exhausted from the day's events. This experience had given us pause for thought about all the stories we'd heard before about mysterious creatures including Bigfoot being in the wilderness of Idaho.

In the morning my wife and I talked more about this experience before going to talk to our kids who were already up watching television in the living room. We had both decided that, for now, it would be best to keep what we had seen to ourselves as not to scare them for future skiing trips. To this day, we have never seen anything like this again but every time we venture out into the wilderness, the ape-like creature is always in the back of our minds.

We can't help but wonder if, on that fateful night, we had stumbled across a true Idaho Bigfoot! Only time will tell. Until then, all we can do is keep exploring and remain open to the possibility that one day we could encounter it again. Who knows what wonders nature holds for us? We certainly won't be giving up anytime soon!

ENCOUNTER #4 Bass Fishing with a Side of Bigfoot

I have been an avid fisherman since I was a young boy - it's always been my favorite pastime and a way for me to escape from the hustle and bustle of life. My friends all share in this passion, so when my buddy and coworker Justin suggested that we go fishing at Swan Falls Dam one late summer evening after work, there was no way I could say no!

It was a Tuesday night, and what had seemed like an incredibly long day at work quickly faded away as soon as we got into Justin's car to head out. We stopped by his house to get our rods, tackle boxes, buckets and coolers before continuing on our journey towards the dam. As soon as we got in the car, I could feel my body begin to relax. Justin and I had been friends since grade school, and I was so happy that he'd been able to get a job at the factory with me on the same shifts; it sure helped having someone there to talk to in order to pass the time doing mundane work.

We drove for about 45 minutes before finally reaching our destination. As soon as we pulled into the parking lot next to Swan Falls Dam, I could feel my excitement level rising. It was a moonlit night with a bright glow across the water's surface and it felt like anything was possible that night. We got out of the car quickly and set up our rods and tackle boxes, eager to get out onto the dock.

The great thing about working second shift is that we got to do things at night without being around a lot of other people, and this night was no different- we had the whole place to ourselves as we had arrived around midnight. Knowing that, we decided that we could fish for about three hours before calling it a day in order to get some rest before work the next morning.

We spent the first hour or so casting our lines into the water and hoping to catch some smallmouth bass. We were both rewarded with a few bites here and there but nothing of any size or significance yet. I was slowly starting to lose hope when something unexpected happened. Out of the corner of my eye, I spotted a large figure walking along the shoreline, looking down into the water as it walked. At first, I thought it was another fisherman but as it got closer I saw that it was much larger than expected. Quickly getting Justin's attention, we could see that this ape-like creature had dark fur covering its body, an ape-like face with a leathery texture and almost human expression on its face like it was surprised we were there.

Justin and I stared in awe at the ape-like creature that had suddenly appeared before us. We guessed it was out looking for fish to eat, but its unexpected appearance had us both rooted to the spot unable to move or make any noise. We watched as it studied us for a few moments before it finally turned around and bolted back to where it had come from in the darkness along the shoreline before disappearing into the night, leaving Justin and me shaken but still mesmerized by what we had seen.

Could this ape-like creature really have been Bigfoot, that mysterious cryptid said to roam these parts? We had both heard about bigfoot over our childhoods and were curious about the creature but neither of us were fully convinced it was real until that night. Stories of Bigfoot sightings in Idaho had been talked about for years, but this experience was different and much more real for us.

As the clock struck 3am, Justin and I finally snapped out of our trance and hastily packed up our rods and tackle boxes. We were both in awe of what we had just seen, and excitedly discussed it as we drove back home. It was hard for either of us to fall asleep that night, so when I saw Justin again at work the next day, we joked about going fishing again that very night so that we could experience something just as incredible once more.

We knew that if we told anyone this story they would never believe us; it was simply too incredible to be true. Ever since then, Justin and I have kept it to ourselves as a special secret between the two of us. We felt privileged to witness such an extraordinary event, and neither of us felt threatened by the ape-like creature. It seemed like it had just been going about its day trying to catch itself a meal - much like most other animals - and didn't seem to mean us any harm.

After our encounter with Bigfoot, Justin and I still continued fishing at the dam and many other favorite places around Idaho. However, we always kept our eyes out for wonder in case we ever saw something as amazing as that ape-like creature again. To this day, we still joke about going fishing at night to experience something just as incredible as what we saw that evening. We remain in awe of the mysterious cryptid said to roam these parts - a reminder of how truly extraordinary our world can be.

ENCOUNTER #5 Lawn Workers Close Encounter with Bigfoot

I had been working as a landscaper for one of the city's wealthiest families for about two years. I was 26, an immigrant from Mexico and I had taken this job to provide for my family back home. Every day, I arrived on time with a smile on my face, ready to work. It was a hot summer day in 2020; I remember because it would be the day that changed me forever.

My friend and co-worker Diego had been working with me since we were teenagers. We took odd jobs together everywhere from construction sites to lawn care businesses until we finally settled at the company where we both currently worked. We always joked around while we worked and often went out of our way to help each other out.

This day, we were working on the owner's yard on the edge of town. Diego and I had just finished mowing the lawn when he asked me if I wanted to take a break. We decided to grab some lunch before continuing with our tasks, so we left the riding mower in the backyard of the estate and went for some burgers at a nearby restaurant. The food was amazing, especially after all of the work we'd put in that morning. On our way back, we stopped at a gas station and purchased a few sodas and waters to get us through the afternoon.

When we returned about an hour later, something felt very off. We both noticed it immediately as soon as we entered into the backyard and my heart skipped a beat. There was one of the trees that we had planted yesterday which was now uprooted and shoved back into the ground with its top down, buried deep enough so that it would stay upright with its roots exposed. Why in the world would someone do this?

We were both baffled by what had happened. All the work we put into planting the tree yesterday appeared to have been undone in a matter of an hour. The owners were not home, and neither were the neighbors. We surveyed our surroundings, but the estate was secluded from the sight of the road and no one seemed to be around.

We examined the uprooted tree further and noticed what looked like scrape marks in the dirt where it had been buried back into place. It didn't look like a tool had done this work; instead, it appeared more like scratch marks from large hands moving dirt to bury it again. There were no footprints in the dirt, but that could be explained because grass surrounded this area, so someone could have done this to the tree while standing in the grass.

We both knew immediately what we were thinking: was someone playing some type of joke on us? Unsure of what to do, we decided it would be best to finish up our remaining lawn work and wait for one of the owners to come home from work so that we could ask them if they had invited anyone else onto the property or had any idea of what happened. We labored for a few more hours in the hot sun and took a break to have a soda and stare at this tree further;

both of us continued to be highly confused about what had happened.

We finished our break and made it through the last two hours before Jim came home from the office. I went to the front door and knocked; we had a great relationship with him, but out of respect I always knocked before going into the house. When he opened the door, he asked how we were doing. We quickly explained what had happened in the backyard and he looked uneasy that we were saying something strange had occurred on his property.

We took Jim to the backyard to show him the tree that had been uprooted and buried back into place again. He was just as confused as us and assured us that he had not told anyone else to do this, nor did he think it was a prank. We showed him the large hand scratch marks in the dirt around the tree and discussed how odd of an occurrence this was. I told Justin that we would purchase a new tree in the morning and replace it.

We thanked Jim for his time and said our goodbyes, then headed home for the evening. On the way back, Diego mentioned that something felt off about the situation. He didn't want to go back to work tomorrow. I tried to reassure him, saying it was no big deal and we'd get it fixed in the morning. After all, we had been working for this family for so long and needed the income. Diego reluctantly agreed, but he still seemed uneasy about it.

The next morning, Diego and I returned to the greenhouse where we had purchased the three trees earlier in the week. Justin, the same worker from before, was there to greet us. We said hello and asked him if he had another tree in stock. He replied that he did and offered to take us out back to get one. As we began walking to the back lot, Justin asked if we were starting another project of planting more trees.

Diego and I both looked at each other and then I told him what had happened - someone had uprooted one of our trees, shoved it into the ground upside down, and buried it there! Justin seemed confused by this news but we filled him in on all the details of the strange event. We bought the replacement tree and Justin, with his good sales skills, suggested we also buy some mesh metal fencing to place around the tree for added security. We agreed that this would help prevent someone from uprooting it again.

We thanked Justin for his help and headed to the property with our new tree and fencing in tow. As we drove away, Diego still seemed uneasy about what had happened the previous day but I reassured him that everything would be alright; after all, we had been working for this family for so long and needed the income. He reluctantly agreed but I could still sense his apprehension as we arrived to replace the uprooted tree.

We arrived back at the family's property and went to the backyard with our shovels in hand. This time, however, we were even more shocked than the day before. Both of the remaining trees had been uprooted and buried upside down in the ground! Our jaws dropped open in awe and terror as we stared at this strange event. Diego quickly bolted back to the truck and shut the door, obviously scared by what he saw.

I was equally scared but equally curious as I went over to take a closer look at all three trees. Sure enough, there were large hand scratch marks in the dirt around each tree exactly where they had been planted back into the ground upside down. As I examined the trees further, that is when I noticed something in the woods that bordered the yard. At first, it was just a glimpse of something; I squinted to see it since the morning sun was coming from that direction and making it difficult to see.

Eventually, I saw it but only from the shoulders up behind a tall patch of weeds. This moment completely shocked me; there was an ape-like creature standing about seven feet tall staring right back at me! Its shoulders were wide and it had a matted fur covering its entire body. Its eyes stared at me with intent and its face seemed almost human but somewhat ape like as well. Its head was large and conical in shape. I froze for a moment and then without warning the creature let out an ear-piercing howl that was so loud I could feel it in my chest from fifty yards away!

I quickly ran back to the truck, yelling to Diego to start the engine. I jumped in and we drove away as fast as we could, trying not to look back. I could tell Diego was scared and confused by my sudden reaction. He asked me what had happened and I told him that I had seen a huge ape-like creature in the woods with human characteristics but much larger than an average person and covered in thick fur.

He knew from the fear in my voice that this was no joke. We sped back towards his house and he invited me inside when we arrived. His wife was away at work for the day and his two children were at school, so it was just us two men alone in his living room trying to figure out what to do. We sat there in silence for a few hours, both of us perplexed and unsure of how to proceed.

We had experienced something so terrifying and otherworldly that we couldn't even begin to explain what it was. After a few hours of discussing the situation, we eventually decided that there was no way we could go back and work at that house anymore. We were getting paid weekly, so we would only lose out on a few days' pay. Although we both loved working for this family, the ape-like creature scared us too much - it simply wasn't worth the risk.

That evening, Justin called me around 6pm and asked what had happened as he now had three trees in his backyard that were uprooted. I hesitated to tell him about the ape-like creature I saw but eventually told him what had happened. He said that I must have been seeing things and there had to be some explanation for the uprooted trees. I told him that I knew what I saw and there was no way we could return to his property. He begged me to reconsider, but out of exhaustion from the day, I told him I had to go and hung up.

Justin tried calling me several times over the next week, but I never answered his calls. Although I felt bad about it, I knew there was nothing he could say that would change my mind. I had seen a seven-foot ape-like creature in Idaho's woods and was too scared to go back. It was something so mysterious and otherworldly that it was entirely beyond our understanding.

Fortunately, we didn't have much trouble finding new lawn care work - it was in high demand at the time and we both quickly found employment at another property. Our new job wasn't as good as our previous one but we knew without hesitation that we would never accept work near Justin's property again.

To this day, we still wonder what the creature was. We concluded that the uprooting of the trees must have been some way of marking its territory. Perhaps it had always been in that area but we were typically in and out of Justin's backyard quickly after mowing. But this week, with us spending a bit more time planting the new trees, it must have felt encroached upon and wanted to scare us away - which it did! We never returned to that property again.

ENCOUNTER #6 A Mysterious Encounter in Boise River WMA

It was the summer of 2009, and I had just turned 34. After nearly a decade working as a farm equipment salesman, I decided to take my annual elk hunting trip in Boise River WMA in Idaho, which was roughly an hour from my house. My wife Sara and I had been married for seven years, but we hadn't started a family yet. We weren't sure if kids were even in our future at that point - this gave me plenty of time to reflect on the kind of life we could have with children. Would I still be able to do these hunting trips that brought me so much joy? Or would it become more enjoyable if I could bring my son or daughter along?

With these thoughts in mind, I set out early that Thursday morning for the four-day weekend I had off from work. Since the hunting ground was only an hour away, I decided to drive there and back each day in order to save on overnight stay costs. I packed up my gear, loaded it into the pickup truck, and poured a nice cup of coffee into my thermos before setting off. The drive was peaceful and quiet - the perfect way to start a hunting trip after so much time spent thinking about life.

Upon arriving at Boise River WMA, I quickly got to work getting ready for the hunt. After gearing up and coming up with a plan for the day, I decided that stalking would be my best bet - that way I could wander from spot to spot and look for an elk walking by.

It was a cool morning, but the weather was perfect for elk hunting so I didn't mind. The first day went by without seeing an elk, although I had made mental note of a few spots where it looked like elk had been traveling through. Once the sun had set, I headed back home - my wife Sara was there eagerly waiting to hear how my day went.

I continued this pattern through day two as well, stalking in the morning and afternoon while taking breaks during the heat of the day to rest up and stay hydrated. Although I didn't see an elk after two days of hunting, I now had a great idea of where to sit for elk on Saturday and Sunday.

Saturday morning came, and it was much colder and windier than I anticipated - although I was still plenty warm, I knew that elk still move in the wind but not as much as they do when it's calmer. This was a bit disappointing since there were only two days left to hunt. Despite the weather, I made my way near a stream that I had spotted previously. It seemed like a good area for elk to pass through, but the entire morning produced nothing. Although I didn't see any elk, I did hear a few making their distinctive bugle calls in the distance - at least I knew there were some around.

I decided to pack up and move to another section of the stream further down for the rest of the afternoon. When I got there, I sat down on the ground in front of a large tree. This spot was perfect because it overlooked the stream, and with the tree and brush to my back, it would not allow the elk to silhouette me against the setting sun as the day went on.

I had my lunch which was super basic - a bag of beef jerky and a protein bar from the gas station I had stopped at earlier that morning. Keeping meals light while hunting helps me prevent being weighed down or potentially upsetting my stomach while in the wilderness. As I ate, my thoughts again returned to what life with children would be like, taking them hunting with me. After all, that is how I learned to hunt when my dad brought me and I could tell it brought him a lot of joy.

My thoughts were interrupted by the sound of a splash of water coming from the stream. I was in a spot where the stream bent, so I couldn't yet see what was making the sound until it rounded the bend. It sounded large, so could this be an elk walking through the stream?

I sat in anticipation as the sound got closer and closer. After a few moments, I could finally begin to make out what it was through the trees leading down to the stream to my right. It was very large but still not in a clearing where I could make out exactly what it was. Being an experienced hunter, I knew that now was the best time to position myself better for a shot in that direction before whatever it was could easily see me move.

I got into a better position, and then used my range finder to pick out a good shooting spot down to the creek. It was 137 yards away, which was an easy shot for my high-powered rifle. I made one last adjustment to my scope and held still, as I waited for the animal in the stream to come within view. What I saw when it finally rounded the corner sent a chill down my spine: standing right before me was a creature that was standing on two legs and walking walking through the creek.

My heart raced as I tried to process what this strange creature could be. Even from 137 yards away, I could tell it was incredibly tall - likely 8 or 9 feet! Its ape-like figure had long arms that went down past its knees, and it was covered in matted fur that was a very dark brown color.

I stayed motionless, my breath held in anticipation as I watched the ape-like creature walk closer and closer. As it emerged from the stream into a clearing, I finally had a good look at its face - and my eyes almost jumped out of my head. It wasn't just ape-like in appearance; there was something about its expression that seemed nearly human with real emotion. No doubt remained in my mind that this wasn't an elk, bear or any other animal I had seen before.

Sasquatch! The thought suddenly came to me - though it hadn't been my first thought when seeing such an unusual creature, having hunted all my life made it easy for me to instantly recognize what I was dealing with. I stayed as still as possible, my heart pounding out of my chest for fear that any sudden movements would startle it and make it notice me. Fortunately, the creature continued its course from right to left, never coming close enough for me to have to worry about that.

Despite having a high-powered rifle in hand, a small part of me still wondered if it would be adequate to do damage against such an ape-like creature that seemed so large and imposing. After all, what sort of fight could I expect from it? All these thoughts ran through my head as I watched the Sasquatch pass by and disappear into the distance as it continued its walk through the clearning.

I sat there processing what had just happened and I was simply amazed by its size and how gracefully it walked through the running water. It made me wonder if there could be another one close by, or even more than that! And also what this thing was doing - perhaps it was simply searching for fish or using the stream as a way to navigate the terrain as it made its way through the wilderness.

I stayed rooted to the spot long after the ape-like creature had faded from my view. My mind raced in wonder with so many unanswered questions on this creature and how amazing it was that I happened to see one. After about 10 minutes, I finally snapped out of the trance and had a decision to make: should I sit here and finish out the last few hours of the evening hunt or should I pack up now so that I could walk back to my truck in the daylight?

I made the decision to head back to my truck, quickly yet cautiously. The walk back was a long one and I couldn't help but feel like I was being watched the entire time. Though it could have just been my imagination running wild, there was something about the thought of ape-like creatures with so many human characteristics possibly tracking me that had the hair on the back of my neck standing up.

In what felt like an eternity, I finally reached my truck safely and took off my heavy outer gear before starting it up and beginning to pull out from the gravel parking lot. As I began to reverse onto the dirt road, I glanced out of my driver's side window towards where I had come walking through - only for my eyes to meet the ape-like figure of a creature staring back at me from about 40 yards away.

At the sight of the ape-like creature standing in front of me, I knew my intuition was right; something had been watching me on my walk back. This sent a chill down my spine to think that this mysterious creature may have been tracking me as I made my way out of the wilderness. Without hesitation, I stepped on it and immediately began driving down the dirt road until finally reaching the highway.

My drive home was a long one, filled with my mind wandering in wonder of the ape-like creature I had just seen. What was it? How many were there? How long had they been here? Where else might they be?

When I arrived home, Sara was sitting on the couch and watching TV. She was surprised to see me at that time since I usually stayed out in the woods until dark – so she hadn't expected me for another two hours. Without much said, I put down my gear and joined her on the couch. She asked if something was wrong and after taking a deep breath I told her what had happened. She seemed highly confused and surprised, but knew that I wasn't lying.

I was worried that she might think I had gone crazy, but Sara has always supported me through anything in life and this situation was no different. For the next several weeks, it was hard for me to sleep peacefully as my mind kept going back to what I had seen. To this day, the experience still remains a mystery to me.

At the time I had decided not to go back for the Sunday hunt and in fact I have not gone back to that location ever to hunt again. It actually took me over two years before I went hunting again, but finally ventured out to different public land in Idaho. My hunting life had changed forever though as I could never be fully at ease when I was hunting for fear of what might be out there and watching me. To this day I'm still not sure what the creature's intent was with me when it followed me to my truck. Perhaps it was just curious about me, or perhaps it meant harm. I'm glad that I made it away safely regardless.

ENCOUNTER #7 Encounter at Freddy's Stack Rock Trail in Idaho

It was the late summer of 2020, and I, John had just reconnected with an old friend from high school - Sara. We had dated briefly during our senior year before she moved away after graduation. Although we had kept in touch sporadically over the years, it wasn't until recently that we truly reconnected. One of our rare phone calls resulted in us deciding to meet up for a hike near where I lived in Idaho.

Sara arrived at my place early on Saturday morning and by 8am we were already headed out towards Freddy's Stack Rock Trail. It was so good to see her again; it felt like no time had passed since the last time saw each other! The car ride was filled with small talk and stories from the past; we talked about our families, our jobs, and even some of the old friends that were still in touch.

We chatted as we walked down the path that lead us deeper into the woods, talking about what had happened since our high school days. I was telling Sara a funny story about what John and I had done in college when out of nowhere we heard a loud crash in the trees to the left of the trail. We both stopped dead in our tracks and turned to look for whatever had made that sound. That's when I saw it - an ape-like creature walking through the trees not far from where we stood.

It seemed like time had stopped as Sara and I just stared at the creature, neither of us able to move or speak. The ape-like figure was enormous; nearly 8 feet tall with long arms and a wide body. It seemed to be aware of us but didn't show any signs of aggression. For what felt like an eternity, we just stared at each other before the ape eventually ambled away further into the forest leaving us in awe.

After it had gone, Sara and I just looked at each other in disbelief. We were both too stunned to speak or move; the ape-like creature had been so surreal that we felt like if it wasn't for the unconditional trust between us, we might've thought that one of us was playing a prank on the other.

We finally snapped out of our trance and began walking back towards my car as fast as we could without running away. Thinking about it now, I don't know why neither of us ran.

Perhaps, deep down we knew that running away would only make it more likely for the ape to attack? In any case, all I wanted to do was get home as soon as possible - so with haste, we both hurriedly made our way back to the car.

On the drive home, neither of us said anything. We were in shock over what had just happened; it felt like we were both trying to process and make sense of the ape-like creature that we had seen walking through the forest. The silence lasted until finally, we reached my place.

As soon as I parked my car and shut off the engine, all I wanted to do was get inside and away from whatever had been out there in the woods. Sara stayed for a bit longer so we could debrief on what had just happened but neither of us had any real answers - only theories. My favorite theory was that the ape-like figure might've been some kind of Bigfoot or even an alien!

Eventually, Sara decided that it was time for her to leave. Before she left, however, she promised me that she would still call me again for another hike - though this time in a different location. We both laughed at the joke; it felt good to make light of our experience after such an intense moment.

We said our goodbyes and I watched her drive off before finally heading inside my home. Even days later, I still couldn't believe what had happened out on Freddy's Stack Rock Trail in Idaho - but it made me curious about all the other people who have seen similar ape-like creatures in the state of Idaho and around the world. Could there be more out there like Bigfoot? I suppose only time will tell.

ENCOUNTER #8 Water Skiing Encounter with Bigfoot

It was a warm summer day in 2014 and my husband, Tyler, our 9 year old daughter Chloe and our 12 year old son Sean and I had decided to take a drive up to Lake Pend Oreille in Idaho. This was our favorite place for waterskiing, so we loaded the truck and boat with all of our swimming gear, snacks, sunscreen and life vests and took off early that morning.

As we drove up into the mountains, we watched the scenery change from rolling hills to dense forests and sparkling blue lakes. We felt like kids ourselves as we took in all of the beauty around us - it felt especially exciting knowing that this would be one of Chloe's first times ever trying out water skiing. When we arrived at the lake's shoreline, Tyler couldn't contain his excitement - he had grown up water skiing with his father back home in Montana and he couldn't wait to teach Chloe.

We took our time setting up the boat, making sure that all of the necessary safety precautions were taken before we got out on the water. Once everything was set, Tyler hopped in the driver seat while Sean and I jumped into the boat with Chloe, who was already wearing her life vest. We enjoyed a few hours of driving around the lake - it was so peaceful to be surrounded by nature and to feel the summer breeze against our faces.

It was getting close to noon and the sun was starting to warm up, so Chloe had become a bit anxious for her chance to go water skiing. Tyler started off slowly, coaching Chloe on how to balance and steer the skiis as he made laps around the lake. After several attempts, she finally managed to get up on the skiis and it almost immediately seemed like second nature to her - no sooner had she gotten up than she wanted to keep going and going!

We all cheered from the boat as we watched Chloe make her way around with increasing confidence and speed. She looked so proud of herself - you could tell that she was really enjoying the moment. We were all having such a great time watching Chloe ski around, it felt like no time had passed at all before we realized that it was already nearing 2pm.

It was then that Tyler suggested we take a break for lunch. He steered the boat to the shoreline, anchoring it in place before I started pulling out sandwiches, chips and waters from our cooler. We all enjoyed the sunny warmth while eating our food together, laughing at how quickly time had flown by since morning.

We were mid-conversation, eating our sandwiches and laughing together in the shade near the shoreline. Suddenly, something strange happened - a rock the size of a grapefruit landed in the water with a loud splash, startling us all. We looked around to see where it had come from but could not find an explanation. Just then, another rock hit near our boat with a big splash.

We were all in shock - standing motionless and speechless as we stared at the ape-like creature in the distant tree line. It was clear that this was no ordinary animal, it towered over us - nearly 8 feet tall and had strong shoulders and long arms that reached past its knees. Its face was leathery and dark, almost human-like in appearance but with a more ape-like texture.

The creature seemed to be peering at us from behind some shrubbery just beyond the edge of the lake and when it noticed us looking back at it, it leaned forward quickly and grabbed another rock which it threw directly our way! The rock flew through air with force so powerful that it sailed right over our boat and landed in the water behind us - at least 20 yards away!

We were all so scared that we could barely move. We just stood there, frozen in disbelief as we watched the ape-like creature standing in the tree line. I had heard stories of Bigfoot sightings in Idaho, but never expected to see one on this day. We were shaken and scared but unable to deny what we were seeing with our own eyes.

Finally, Tyler snapped out of his trance and told me to start pulling up the anchor while he started the boat engine. In that short moment of hesitation, two more rocks landed near our boat! As soon as I got the anchor up and into the boat, Tyler put the engine on full throttle and headed across the water towards the boat launch.

We made it back to the boat launch in about 10 minutes, and as we sped away I looked back towards the shoreline. To my amazement, the ape-like creature was still standing there watching us drive away. We were all in awe of what had just happened and silently thanked our lucky stars that none of us had been hurt by any of the rocks thrown at us.

When we arrived at the boat launch, luckily nobody was putting a boat in at the time so I hopped out of the boat and backed up the truck with the trailer. Tyler navigated the boat onto the trailer and secured it before hopping into the driver's seat. We quickly did our final checks on the boat making sure everything was in order before speeding off.

The ape-like creature had left a lasting impression on all of us, and even though it was an intense experience none of us would ever forget the thrill we felt when making eye contact with this mysterious being. We drove away in a solemn silence, trying to comprehend what we had just witnessed and wondering if any other Idahoans have seen such a creature.

Chloe was still shaking from the intense experience when I began to explain what we had just seen. I told her that I wasn't sure what it was, but that I was glad we were safe now. After a few moments of silence, I decided to come clean and tell her about the stories of Bigfoot - an ape-like creature with high intelligence that some believe has yet to be discovered by modern science.

I said that while I couldn't be sure, it certainly felt like a one-in-a lifetime experience. Chloe then asked why the ape-like creature had been throwing rocks at us. Doing my own processing on the matter, I explained that likely we had been encroaching on its territory and it had been trying to scare us away. I noted that while it had the power to hit our boat directly with the rocks, several of them had flown over it. This seemed to suggest a higher level of intelligence as it was clearly aware that having the rocks land near us would be enough to frighten us off without actually risking harming us.

We made our drive back home with Chloe continuing to ask questions, and I did my best to come up with answers – though I didn't know the answers either. When we finally arrived back home and parked the vehicle, I looked into the back seat at both of our kids and told them that I loved them. I said that it is usually not a good idea to keep secrets, but this was one of those rare times when it was best to keep the experience between us four.

I was truly worried that my kids would be teased at school if they ran around telling classmates that they had seen Bigfoot. To ensure their safety, I made them promise not to tell anyone else about what happened. The children agreed without hesitation. With that in mind, we all sat in the truck for a few moments taking comfort in the knowledge that we were safe and sound.

From then on, none of us spoke much about what had happened out on the lake. It seemed to be something too incredible to put into words – like a dream that would quickly fade away with each passing day. Though I don't think any of us will ever forget that warm summer day when our paths crossed with an ape-like creature from Idaho's mysterious forests.

ENCOUNTER #9 Mysterious Sounds in Ponderosa State Park

It was late summer of 1997, and my best friend Bill and I decided to take a much needed break from our busy lives by going camping in Ponderosa State Park, Idaho. We had been friends since early childhood; growing up just down the road from each other we would spend our summers biking around and exploring our neighborhood, doing our best to stay out of trouble. We were looking forward to some quality time together amidst the beauty of nature and catching up on our lives - although now living just on the other side of town, we only saw each other a few times a year.

It was Memorial Day weekend so we had an extra day off from work and I picked him up in my beat-up minivan shortly after I got off work. Immediately, we started talking and teasing each other as if not a day had gone by since we last saw each other - the drive was fun and we were both so excited for this time together.

When we arrived at the park, it was like stepping into a paradise of lush green trees and rolling hills. We grabbed our gear and headed out to the camp sites, finally settling on one beneath a large ponderosa pine tree near Payette Lake. One of the best parts about this spot was that it offered us a great view for fishing and swimming - two activities Bill and I were especially looking forward to during our stay.

As it began to get dark, I took some time gathering firewood while Bill finished setting up the camp site. Once everything was ready, I started the fire and we gathered around it as we prepped for our three night stay - adjusting sleeping bags, roasting marshmallows, sharing stories from our childhood, and laughing until we couldn't laugh any more. We also cracked open a few beers from the local brewery that I had brought with me - they were the perfect way to cap off a long day of travelling and setting up camp.

As night settled in around us, all we could hear was the gentle lapping of lake water and the stars above us glittering bright. With nothing but the pure beauty of nature surrounding us, it was hard not to feel completely at peace. After talking for hours, Bill and I drifted off into a deep sleep beneath the canopy of trees - little did I know what awaited us in just a few short hours...

It was around 2:30 in the morning when I heard a strange sound coming from the distance. At first, my mind was foggy and I thought it must have been an effect of the six beers I had drank during the night - but then it came again. It sounded like a long howl, unlike anything I'd ever heard before.

I tried to clear my mind and listen intently, trying to make sense of this unusual noise. Could it be a wolf or coyote that just sounded different than others I had heard in the past? Something about it seemed so unique - as if nothing could possibly compare to this mysterious call echoing through the night air.

A chill ran down my spine as I lay there in the stillness of night, trying to identify the source of this mysterious howling. After what seemed like an eternity, the sound stopped and all that remained was an eerie silence. I stayed awake for some time afterward, my heart pounding from being so abruptly awoken.

When morning eventually came, I was up first to prepare us a hot cup of coffee. It wasn't until nearly an hour later that Bill finally emerged from his slumber. I asked him if he had heard anything strange last night while he was sleeping and he said no - not surprising considering the amount of beer he finished off during our evening around the campfire.

After breakfast, Bill and I decided to do some fishing at the lake. We were targeting trout so that we could have a nice meal for dinner. The day was warm and perfect, with blue skies above us and a gentle breeze blowing through the camp site - it was hard not to feel completely relaxed in this peaceful environment. We fished from shore for a few hours, catching a few smaller trout right away that we threw back but managed to mix in four keeper Trout by mid afternoon.

We decided to head back to camp for a light lunch, clean the fish, and then go for a hike before coming back for dinner. As we made our way up the trail to our campsite, I couldn't help but think back to the eerie howling I had heard in the night. Bill said he was sure I just had heard a wolf and continued on with our day, but I couldn't shake the feeling that those sounds weren't of a normal animal in Idaho.

Once we made it back to camp, we cooked up some lunch and quickly set out for our hiking excursion. Despite my lingering thoughts of what could have caused that strange sound, nothing seemed amiss and so we genially ventured into the woods. We spent hours exploring around, taking in all of Idaho's natural beauty until eventually heading back as night began to fall once more.

As the sun set and I began to grow increasingly nervous about what could be lurking in the night, Bill laughed at my childish behavior. Deep down I was scared from our previous experience with the unknown howling sound in the dark of the night, but thankfully we were able to make it back safely to camp without any further incident.

We enjoyed a delicious meal of freshly caught trout and had a few beers before starting to make plans for tomorrow's adventure. We got into some small talk about our day when suddenly, I heard the same mysterious sound in the distance that I had heard before. I told Bill to stay still and listened intently - sure enough it came again: a mysterious calling out like nothing I had ever heard before. Bill heard it too - it was the same sound from the night before. We both looked at each other, sharing a feeling of trepidation and confusion.

As we started to settle down for the evening, I couldn't help but feel a sense of unease in the air. We both heard an eerie sound coming from somewhere in the distance and although Bill shrugged it off as just a wolf, I was not so sure. The howling kept getting louder and then stopped abruptly - it felt like whatever had been making that noise was now closer than before.

Bill thought there was nothing to worry about and went to sleep soon after, however I could not get myself to rest despite my exhaustion. Every few minutes I would wake up thinking I heard something again, but thankfully all remained silent until around 2:30 in the morning when suddenly I was greeted with a different sound - one of deep thuds, almost as if something was hitting wood. It only happened a few times and then stopped altogether.

By the time morning arrived I had hardly gotten an hour of sleep in total for the night. Bill seemed oddly unfazed by the events from the previous evening and so we decided to get up and start our day as planned; though my mind still lingered on what creature could have caused these sounds.

The thought had actually crossed my mind that it was a bigfoot, as I had run across a few shows about them over the years and would casually watch them here and there. These shows often described bigfoots making howling sounds as well as wood knocks to communicate with one another. Were these mysterious sounds caused by such a creature?

I didn't dare bring up the idea of bigfoot to Bill, as he had already laughed off the idea that it was anything but a wolf. Nevertheless, I knew speculating about what we heard in the night wouldn't do us any good. What mattered now was exploring the area and enjoying our last night camping. We both packed water and snacks for lunch on the trail and discussed the special steak, shrimp, and pasta dinner we had planned for when we returned that evening.

Our afternoon of hiking was exciting; however at one point I trailed slightly behind Bill as we went up an incline, and I thought I caught a glance of something off to our left off the trail. I stopped and froze for a minute before telling Bill to stop as well. We sat there in silence for a few moments, but then he laughed and said I must be going crazy -- I didn't see anything else and so it seemed my mind was playing tricks on me.

As it began to get dark, we headed back to camp for our final dinner. I now felt an air of anticipation for the evening ahead. Would we hear those noises again? After a quiet meal, Bill and I settled into our sleeping bags and I sat up for some time in my sleeping bag just waiting for the sounds again. But nothing out of the ordinary was heard on our final night - all remained silent until morning came.

We decided to pack up camp before sunrise so that we would make good time getting back home. As we walked back to our vehicle, I tried to hide my nervousness better and once we were driving out of the park I finally felt at ease. We stopped by Bill's house just after noon on Sunday and I went home. After unpacking, I decided to do some online research about bigfoots, and their sounds.

I was becoming increasingly convinced that what we heard at our campsite the two nights were indeed from a Bigfoot! I found out more information about bigfoot and their sightings in Idaho, as well as reports from other witnesses who had heard similar loud thuds and wood knocks. While listening to audio recordings of these noises, I noticed that they were nearly identical to what we heard -- it seemed clear to me that this ape-like creature had been around us both nights.

As I continued to reflect on what had happened during our stay, my thoughts wandered back to when we were hiking. I recalled that, as I trailed slightly behind Bill on an incline, something caught my eye off to the left side of the trail. When I got a better look, it seemed like an ape-like figure was standing there watching us! It all happened so quickly and then vanished almost immediately. Could this have been a bigfoot?

It was hard for me to say for certain; however, I could not shake the feeling that this might have been the same creature whose noises we heard in the night -- a reminder of its presence watching us from afar. This thought stayed with me long after our camping trip was over.

I was left with the mystery of whether I had seen a bigfoot in Idaho that weekend. One thing was certain: it had been an unforgettable experience. Ever since then, my mind has been open to the possibility of an undiscovered ape-like creature living out there in the Idaho wilderness. Now when I see any shows about Bigfoot on TV, I'm much more engaged and eager to learn more.

This camping trip changed me; it opened my eyes up to a world beyond what science can explain and left me with countless questions. What exactly did Bill and I hear during our stay? Was it really a Bigfoot? How many of them are out there roaming around in the woods? All these thoughts keep coming back to me and I'm sure that one day soon, we will have the answers. Until then, Idaho's Bigfoot remains shrouded in mystery.

ENCOUNTER #10 A Creature that Has Been Lurking for Years

It had been an eventful day on the farm — my father and I had finished up our work, checking all of the fences out in the fields. We'd been working hard since early that morning and it was now quite late in the evening, with a full moon hanging low in the sky. The night was unusually still and quiet — so much so that you could hear a pin drop from miles away.

We set off for home on my dad's old truck, bumping down the dirt road towards our ranch house at the end of it. We were both tired from a long day's work but we still had one last thing to do before we could call it a night — check on one of our herds of cattle that was still grazing in the hills.

I'm 17 and a senior in high school. I've always been an ambitious student, dreaming of the day when I can head off to college and pursue my dreams of becoming an agronomist. I was born and raised on my family farm and spend most days helping out with the family business while also working hard at school. I'm very close with my father — he has supported me ever since I expressed interest in agronomy, encouraging me to reach for the stars.

My ambition has taken me far beyond the boundaries of our ranch — I've explored all over Idaho, learning about its diverse wildlife, plants, geology and much more. This passion for nature is one that both my father and I share, which is why we get along so well. It was getting darker as we drove slowly down this winding road, meandering through the dense forest of ponderosa pines that surrounded us.

My dad and I hadn't said a word to each other for quite some time; we were both lost in our own thoughts when suddenly, something caught my eye on the side of the road. At first I thought it might have been a deer or maybe even one of our cows, but as I looked closer, it didn't seem like any animal I had ever seen before. It stood tall, upright on two legs — a creature with fur covering its body.

Dad stopped the truck and we jumped out in awe and shock trying to get a better view, but all we could hear was heavy footsteps running away deep into the woods. The creature seemed as surprised to see us — it felt like time had frozen while dad and I just stared at each other for minutes on end.

I asked my dad what it was and he said he was not sure, all he got a brief view of it but it seemed tall and to be walking on two legs. He wondered if someone was trespassing on our property, but this didn't seem right as we were so far away from town that this would really not make sense. After a moment, dad said to get back into the truck so we could finish our check of the herd.

As we finished our drive down the road, we were relieved to find that the herd was doing well. However, I couldn't shake the strange feeling in my body that we were being watched. We got back into the truck and Dad said it was time for us to head home — Mom had dinner ready for us.

To get home, we had to drive back up the gravel road where we had just seen the mysterious creature. Dad told me to grab the rifle from off of the back window, just in case we saw it again. He seemed angry at thought of someone trespassing on our property without permission and kept driving slowly with his headlights turned up bright as it had gotten darker now.

We drove cautiously through those winding roads of the dense forest, with the loaded rifle on my lap. My dad was keeping his eyes peeled for any signs of the mysterious figure that we had seen earlier while I tried to remain calm and composed despite my fear.

As the truck slowly made its way up the narrow mountain road, I strained my gaze in hopes of catching a glimpse of whatever it was that we had seen before. Then just as we rounded a slight curve near where we had spotted the creature before, our bright headlights illuminated something standing right in front of us in the middle of the road — it was definitely not an ordinary animal!

We were both in shock as we gazed upon the ape-like creature standing before us. It was an incredible sight — a huge figure, resembling a large man wearing a gorilla costume. However, after quick examination it became clear that no human could be this large — it was nearly 8 feet tall! Its face had a human-like expression of surprise and its massive arms were built like a bodybuilder's, but much longer. Its legs were like tree trunks for size and it just stood there like a "deer in the headlights" for about 10 to 15 seconds.

Both the creature and ourselves were processing what to do in this moment — me briefly thinking of raising the rifle to it before realizing that it was so human-like that I could not shoot it. The creature seemed to sense my hesitation, as if its ape-like eyes held some form of understanding or knowledge. Abruptly, it turned away and quickly disappeared into the surrounding darkness of the forest. Its departure felt almost like an act of instinctual decision making, as if it had been through this situation before.

As the ape-like being moved away from us, I noticed how quick and agile it was with ease. Its stride was almost unnatural, suggesting that this ape-like creature had adapted to its environment as an ape but had developed a movement that was far beyond that of any ape.

My dad and I looked at each other in disbelief. We both knew what we had just seen — a Bigfoot, the ape-like creature reported to inhabit certain areas of Idaho. After a few moments more of shock, my dad uttered the words, "Let's get out of here," and sped us down the dirt road back to the farmhouse where Mom was waiting for us.

When we walked inside, Mom had just finished putting the fried chicken on the table when she turned to see us enter the house. She could immediately sense something was out of the ordinary with our expressions and asked if we had seen a ghost. Dad laughed and said that actually it was something much more amazing - we had just seen Bigfoot!

We went on to describe what we had seen to her while we ate dinner. We told her about the ape-like creature, its incredible size, and human-like expression. We described how quickly and agile it was with ease as it moved away from us. Mom listened intently until we had finished our story - her eyes wide in disbelief!

We all just sat there in silent wonder for a few moments after Dad spoke. He said he thought had seen this creature before – that over the years of owning the farm, he had often felt like he was being watched while tending to the cattle, and even occasionally spotted something in the distance but could never get a good look at what it was. This started shortly after getting the farm, but he dismissed it as some other animal.

Mom and I exchanged glances with each other in disbelief, considering how much these sightings must have weighed on Dad's mind over these past years. We asked him if anything else happened during these times, and Dad said he only remembered feeling an intense chill across his body, like someone or something was watching him.

He then went on to tell us of other people in the area that had reported similar sightings. Several of them had claimed they saw an ape-like creature walking around or lurking near their farm animals and homes. Although these stories seemed farfetched, we couldn't deny what we just saw right before our very eyes - a Bigfoot in Idaho!

Dad's words made me feel a bit relieved that we were seemingly safe from the ape-like creature. After all, if this Bigfoot had been lurking around our farm for years and never acted aggressively towards us or taken any of our cows, then it must not be a harm to us. We reasoned that perhaps it was finding other sources of food like deer, elk, and fish in the nearby river; maybe it just liked our property best for living.

This made sense to me but I couldn't help but still feel a tinge of fear in my stomach when I thought about this ape-like creature being so close to us for so long without our knowledge. Dad seemed to pick up on my nervousness and quickly added that if it had wanted to hurt us, it surely would have done so already.

Ever since that day I saw the ape-like creature, I have been on heightened alert when working around our farm. Although I have never seen it again, there have been several occasions where I felt like I was being watched. Whenever this happened, I would remind myself of what my dad had said about the creature not being harmful since it hadn't in the past. While this thought did help to calm me down some, a part of me still worried that if the Bigfoot became desperate for food, it could easily attack us and we wouldn't stand a chance against its superior strength and size.

I completed high school and went to college for agronomy—the science of soil management and crop production. Now, I'm fully engaged in my profession and spend most of my time visiting farms across the state, consulting with farmers on ways to best manage their crops and soil. This often leads me down backroads and secluded areas.

When I'm behind the wheel, I sometimes forget all about the ape-like creature that we saw so many years ago. But other times, especially when the sun is starting to set, thoughts of it come creeping into my mind again. Will I ever see a Bigfoot again?

ENCOUNTER #11 Our Family's Unforgettable Month

I was born and raised on a small farm in the state of Idaho. This land had been in my family for generations, passed down through the years to us. My parents, two older brothers, and I worked hard to maintain the farm and keep it running smoothly. We were content with our lives here; no one ever seemed out of place or strange until one summer evening when something odd happened.

My brothers and I often played together in the barn that sat next to our house - it felt almost like our own little playhouse on the farm! It was early summertime and the sun had just begun to dip below the horizon when my mom noticed something outside from her spot at the kitchen window while she was cooking dinner that night. She saw a figure standing in the shadows near our barn, so she called my dad to come into the kitchen and right when he arrived, it had gone behind the barn. He immediately went outside to check it out.

When Dad came back inside, his face was pale and he looked completely shaken up. He said that he had seen a large ape-like creature scurry away from our property moments before his arrival. Its body was covered in fur, and it moved quickly like a wild animal would. None of us spoke for several minutes; we were too stunned by what we heard to say anything. We all tried to make sense of the situation, but none of us could think of an explanation as to what kind of creature this could be — or why it was near our property.

The next few days seemed surreal as we adjusted to the news my parents had shared with us about the mysterious figure on our farm. We kept looking out the windows and doors, expecting to see it again at any moment. But a week went by without any further incident — until one night when it was unfortunately my turn to see the creature.

I had just gone to bed and was about to doze off when I had a strange sense that I was being watched. The door to my room was closed, so it couldn't have been one of my brothers. Then

I felt like it was something outside of my window. When I opened my eyes, there it was: an ape-like creature staring right back at me through the glass! Its eyes were so intense that they could almost penetrate into your soul. Its face was full of curiosity and wonder, like it wanted to know more about me but couldn't quite find the words to ask. We locked eyes for what felt like an eternity.

I didn't move; I was so consumed by the creature's presence that I couldn't bear to startle it away. There was something almost hypnotic about its gaze, as if it were trying to tell me something without words. We stayed still and locked eyes for what felt like an eternity before, suddenly, it slowly turned away from my window and crept back into the darkness of the night.

I jumped out of bed and ran to my parents' room, telling them what had happened in a flurry of words. Under normal circumstances they would have thought I was dreaming, but since they had both seen a strange ape-like figure on our farm only a week prior, they knew this wasn't just some made up story.

For the next few nights I chose to sleep on the floor in my parents' bedroom, just as an extra layer of reassurance. Surprisingly, I felt only a mild apprehension when thinking back on that night — not fear, but rather compassion and curiosity. After all, the creature hadn't looked at me with aggression or hatred; it seemed almost gentle. I could still feel its presence lingering in my thoughts long after it had gone.

It had been nearly a month since the ape-like creature was seen on our farm. My brothers and I were in the barn playing cops and robbers, with me being the prisoner. They had just finished pretend handcuffing me when they started leading me to the back of the barn from outside. That is when all of us saw it: about 120 yards away, near our fence line, stood an ape-like figure.

We all froze, unable to move or speak; fear had taken over our bodies like a tide coming in. My invisible handcuffs came off immediately, but I was too afraid to do anything else. The ape-like creature seemed oblivious to us and after a few moments it slowly walked along our property line without ever looking in our direction. We watched as it left quietly, disappearing into the brush just as quickly as it had arrived.

We were all still in a state of shock when we heard my dad's truck coming up the road from town. He had gone for some parts earlier that day and his return signaled an opportunity to tell someone about what we had just seen. We decided to go back inside and fill our mom in on the ape-like creature, then waited for dad's return so we could let him know about this too.

When dad finally arrived, our description of the ape-like creature appeared to take him aback — not out of disbelief, but rather surprise. We had described it as being at least 8 feet tall and walking on two feet. When he had seen this creature a month prior it was night and his sighting wasn't nearly as detailed as ours since we saw it during the middle of the day.

We described the ape-like figure as being covered in what looked like reddish-brown fur and having a broad, ape-like face with small eyes. Its body was bulky, but well proportioned, and it seemed to be scanning the area for something. We could also make out large hands at the end of its long arms that were moving slowly from side to side.

My dad quickly concluded that he wanted us three boys to stay together anytime we were playing outside, and we always followed his instruction for the year or so after. Thankfully, it was something that never became a problem again; none of us ever saw the creature or had any odd situations happen ever again. However, our entire family now had first-hand experience with this ape-like figure — myself having seen it twice.

We all shared stories and details about our separate encounters with the ape-like figure, becoming more certain than ever that what we'd seen was real and not just an imagined figment of our imaginations. We quickly came to the conclusion that this ape-like creature must have been doing something in the area, otherwise why would it be there?

Naturally, word spread around town as soon as news got out about our sighting, prompting locals and friends to tease us about it. Some of the teasing was really bad and it caused us a lot of grief at times, but we always stuck together and confirmed what we had seen. In hindsight I wish we would have kept this experience to just our family instead of sharing it with others.

Still, it has become a story that we tell often, recounting the ape-like figure in detail to others who are just as amazed and curious as us. We all agree that what we saw was definitely something out of the ordinary and hope to this day that someday we might get another glimpse at it again. Our own personal experience with the ape-like creature has become a part of our family's history, and we're not alone in experiencing something like this. In fact, there are quite a few sightings of bigfoot being reported in Idaho each year — all adding to the mystery and intrigue of this ape-like creature.

Who knows what else is out there waiting to be discovered? We may never know, but that's part of the mystery and fun of it all. So, if you ever find yourself in Idaho and think you hear a strange sound or see something out of the ordinary, keep your eyes open — you never know what might be lurking nearby! Who knows - maybe it'll be one of those ape-like creatures that we've heard so much about!

ENCOUNTER #12 The Sheriff's Nighttime Encounter

It was the summer of 2018, and I had been Sheriff for three years in my small Idaho town. It wasn't a glamorous job by any means, but it paid the bills and kept me busy enough that I couldn't complain. Most nights were uneventful - patrolling the same streets over and over again and making sure everyone stayed safe.

But one night in particular has stuck with me all these years later, because on this night something entirely unexpected happened. It all started when I got a call from a trailer park on the edge of town; the residents there were reporting strange incidents that had been occurring around their property lately. Rocks were hitting some of the trailers at night, things were moving around, and some even said they heard loud noises coming from outside their homes late at night.

Naturally, I was skeptical - but as a Sheriff it was my duty to investigate any suspicious activity. So I headed over to the trailer park and met up with three of its residents: an elderly woman by the name of Mrs. Johnson, her grandson Jake, and his best friend, Sam. They were all understandably scared and told me that they had been seeing mysterious figures around their trailer, particularly late at night - but they never could get a good enough look to make out who or what it was.

We decided to take a walk around the trailer park, just to see if we could catch a glimpse of this figure. As we were walking, Mrs. Johnson suddenly pointed out several marble-sized rocks near the back side of her trailer which faced a treeline nearby. She stated that for the last several nights she had heard rocks hitting her trailer - and it was definitely strange and concerning behavior.

I began to investigate further, asking them if they had seen or heard anything else that seemed out of place. Jake and Sam both shook their heads but then Mrs. Johnson looked up at the treeline with hesitation in her eyes and said something about hearing strange noises coming from there late at night as well - though she never saw anything.

I had my suspicions at this point and decided to take a look for myself. I headed towards the treeline and told them to go back inside of the trailer while I checked out the area. So, I ventured into the woods on a narrow path that seemed more like something animals rather than people would use. It was pitch black, so I took out my flashlight and kept exploring further into the trees.

At first, it didn't seem like there was anything out of place. I thought perhaps I might run into a homeless person camping out in these woods as an explanation for what could have been going on in the area. However, after about 10 minutes of searching, I heard a loud noise coming from my right side - about 30 feet away from the small path. I pointed my flashlight in that direction, and to my shock, I saw an ape-like creature with long brown fur covering its body, standing there and staring straight at me! It must have been over seven feet tall.

Instinctively, my hand went to my sidearm. As soon as it touched the weapon, the ape-like creature took an aggressive step towards me. Now I could see it more clearly; it had come out from behind the shrubs and its size was both impressive and incredibly intimidating. It seemed as if it knew what a gun was and its behavior immediately changed when it saw me reach for my pistol.

Fear filled me like a wave crashing over me - this animal was far bigger than I had anticipated and it seemed so human, its face now was of anger rather than surprise when I had initially caught sight of it. Realizing that my move to my gun had angered it and the fact that this pistol would likely not do much harm to a creature this size anyway, I snapped the button back to secure my gun and showed the creature the palm of my open hand as if to show it that I no longer presented any harm to it. Immediately its body language changed into a more relaxed stance but it still stared at me with curiosity.

I couldn't believe what I had just witnessed. The ape-like creature that I had encountered was more than likely a bigfoot - an ape-like creature many people have heard of but never thought they would ever actually see in the wild. Standing there, all I could do is stand in awe of what I was seeing. It seemed almost prehistoric, like something straight out of a movie. After looking at it for a few moments, I took a few steps back slowly, and the creature stayed put; it appeared to be more inquisitive than anything else.

I let out a sigh of relief as I watched the ape-like creature slowly turn away from me and begin to make its way back into the woods, disappearing into the night while I could still hear it walking on two legs. It was at that moment that I realized what I had seen - a bigfoot! As my heart rate began to slow down and my shock began to subside, my mind went over all of the details about this encounter. The ape-like creature had been much bigger than I anticipated and seemed so human, with its face displaying anger rather than surprise when I initially caught sight of it.

I slowly started walking back to the trailer home where the woman lived, feeling an overwhelming sense of relief with every step I took. As I walked, I tried to further process what had just happened - the fact that I was safe, the fact that the creature seemed to pose no harm to me until I reached for my gun and what I was going to say to the woman.

I arrived back at the woman's trailer and knocked on the door. When she answered, I put a smile to my face as I remembered my training - it was important for me to always remain calm when speaking to people in order to keep them feeling safe and at ease. She asked if I wanted to come in for a cup of coffee and I gladly accepted.

As soon as I sat down on her couch, she poured me a cup of coffee and asked if I had found anything during my search. My heart began racing again as I tried to think of what story I should tell her - did I really want to tell her that there was an ape-like creature living in her backyard? After taking a deep breath, I quickly fabricated a story that I had seen something that I thought might have been a bear, but that I only got a glimpse of it and scared it off further into the woods. Part of me felt like this was a very reasonable white lie as I was not sure how this woman would react if I told her about the ape-like creature that I had just encountered.

As I finished my cup of coffee, we made small talk and she thanked me for coming out to look for whatever had been causing the disturbance in her backyard. After saying our goodbyes, I began walking away from her trailer home with an overwhelming sense of relief. That night, as my heart rate slowly returned to normal and my shock began to subside.

I drove back into town in a daze, trying to process all that I had just seen. I stopped off at the local supermarket parking lot, a place us officers often went when we needed a break or wanted to meet up. Sure enough, after about 10 minutes, Sam pulled in and asked me how my night was going. Feeling kind of humored by my situation, I jokingly told Sam that I had scared a bigfoot away from an elderly lady's house in the trailer park. We both laughed at the absurdity of it all – it felt good to laugh after such an ordeal – but deep down inside I knew what I had seen was no joke.

I thanked my lucky stars that there were no further reports from the woman or the trailer park about unexplained sightings, strange happenings, or rocks being thrown at houses. I was convinced that although I hadn't posed a threat to the ape-like creature, it had decided it would be best to move on and find a more secluded place to live in order to avoid being spotted again. After all, these creatures have managed to go undetected for so many years; it's only natural that they would want to remain hidden and out of harm's way.

ENCOUNTER #13 A Garden Visited by an Ape Like Creature

It was a beautiful spring morning in the countryside of Idaho. The sun was shining and the birds were singing, as I worked on my small garden. I had just retired at 65 years old, after spending 20+ years married to my now ex-wife. We had grown apart over time, so it wasn't a surprise to anyone when we decided to part ways. Now living alone with my little house and land on the outskirts of town, I found solace in tending to my garden.

I had planted potatoes, onions and four rows of sweet corn - but each day seemed to bring more disappointment than joy as every morning I would find that some of my vegetables had gone missing overnight. At first, I thought maybe it was deer or rabbits, but I had seen neither around my land. After two weeks of this perplexing mystery, I finally decided to put up a four-foot tall chicken wire fence around the perimeter of the garden in hopes that whatever was eating my vegetables would stay away for good.

The following day, I was in the garden again, weeding and watering my vegetables. While I worked, however, I noticed an incredible stench coming from the woods behind my house. It smelled like a swamp - like mud and decay churned up by recent rains and winds. The smell was so intense that it made me retch after just an hour of being outside. With no other option, I went inside to work on some things until the scent had passed.

Little did I know at the time, that this odor was actually coming from something much more mysterious than just stagnant water or decomposing animals. As the sun started to set and darkness slowly crept into view, I heard what sounded like loud footsteps passing by my window. When I peered outside, however, there was nothing there. It was a strange set of occurrences and sent chills down my spine. Nevertheless, I went about the rest of my night as normal - making a nice meal for myself and watching a few hours of television to pass the time in my lonely existence. Little did I know that when morning arrived all would be revealed...

The next morning I made breakfast and had coffee while sitting on my back porch. Thankfully, the musty swamp-like stench from before was gone, so the day promised to be much more pleasant than the one prior. Excitement coursed through me as I thought of getting back to working in my garden. Instinctively, a feeling of dread washed over me - I hoped there wouldn't be any additional vegetables missing this time.

When I finished my breakfast, I walked over to my garden and immediately noticed that something was off. It was as if it had been completely destroyed! Every single row of vegetables had been trampled on, with no sign of the plants or flowers I'd planted just yesterday. In disbelief, I wondered what could have done this? Sure, there were plenty of local wildlife like squirrels, rabbits and big game animals such as deer and elk in the area - even a few bears too. But then something felt strange - the fence around the perimeter was still standing tall and the door inside was shut tight. What kind of creature would do this? The answer soon became clear...

I went inside of the fence, my heart racing with fear. All around me were massive ape-like footprints - each one measuring approximately fourteen inches in length! I had never seen anything like this before and couldn't believe what was happening. As I leaned closer to inspect them, it became clear that these prints were not of any ordinary creature. The five toes on each footprint indicated an ape-like creature that walked upright - much different than other animals like bears or deer who walk flat-footed.

The realization of what had happened to my garden slowly dawned on me, sending a chill down my spine. I had been standing in the very same place where some kind of ape-like creature had been just a few hours earlier. In shock, I picked up my gardening tools and put them away in the garage before going inside my house to process the situation. Sitting there for a few hours, I couldn't help but think about what this creature could be and how it was connected to the terrible stench from yesterday that had now vanished along with the loud footsteps outside last night.

An uncomfortable feeling settled into my chest as I began piecing together all of these events - it seemed like something out of a horror movie! With my curiosity piqued, I decided to conduct some research online and discovered that people had been reporting ape-like creatures in the state of Idaho for years, with the most recent sighting being just a few weeks ago! Could this be the same type of creature that had visited my garden?

I was determined to find out more about the ape-like creature that had visited my garden, so I conducted some research online and learned that people often reported a terrible stench associated with Bigfoot. Just imagine a creature that was human-like but lived outside and didn't have access to soap or a shower - it certainly could smell terrible!

Eager to uncover the truth, I decided to take pictures of the footprints in my garden. There was only one full set left that I hadn't accidentally stepped on already during my inspection. After taking the pictures, however, I wasn't sure what to do next. Calling the police seemed pointless; they would just laugh at me if I told them about these ape-like creatures.

So, I turned to the internet once again and found a few different Sasquatch researchers online. I sent them my pictures and both of them said they believed the prints to be those of Bigfoot. This was all the validation I needed! With this newfound knowledge, I had an even greater appreciation for the mysterious ape-like creature that had roamed through Idaho.

I was terrified by the thought of having a Bigfoot living near my rural home. I asked the Sasquatch researchers for advice on how to make it leave, and they both suggested not replanting my destroyed garden for at least a month or two and keeping any food or garbage away from places that could be accessed by this ape-like creature. I followed their advice, letting the destroyed patch of land sit until spring before finally replanting in hopes that the creatures would have moved onto an easier food source.

By mid-summer, all of my plants were still intact with no more vegetables missing, which gave me some confirmation that the Bigfoot had gone away. The footprints left behind were proof enough that something mysterious had come into my garden, and I believe it was indeed a Bigfoot. Although I never saw the creature myself, these events have me convinced that for those few days I had an ape-like creature living near my home.

ENCOUNTER #14 A Hairy Train Ride Through Idaho

I had been working the BNSF railway line for 17 years, and while I had seen some strange things on my travels back and forth across the country, nothing could have prepared me for what I saw that fateful day. My coworker Brad and I were both railway engineers working aboard the same locomotive train. We had known each other since he started at BNSF six years prior; even though I was almost a decade older than him, we had become quite good friends.

We made good money with our jobs at BNSF but also enjoyed the travel that this type of work provided. However, four years before, my wife and I had our first child and now it was much harder to be away from home. It was late October of 2010 when we set out on our trip that went through Idaho.

This week, we were supposed to be back home by Friday afternoon and I really hoped there would be no issues on the trip. We had been planning a birthday party for our daughter that weekend and I was looking forward to seeing my family again and celebrating with them after being away from home for so long. Brad knew how important this was to me, so he was determined to do everything in his power to make sure we returned in time.

As we continued our journey through Idaho, Brad and I had the usual conversation topics between us. We talked about our common interests such as hunting, fantasy football and other outdoor activities. We also talked about our families back home and how much we were looking forward to being able to spend time with them again in a few days.

We chatted away for hours until eventually we started getting closer to our destination for the evening. We were going through mountain country, and I always enjoyed when the tracks ran near where we could see the snow-capped mountains. The sun was setting, and it was a beautiful sight as it faded behind the peak of one of them. Seeing cows in the fields in Idaho was common, so that wasn't anything out of the ordinary.

Suddenly, out of the corner of my eye I saw something standing on the side of the railway track up ahead that caught my attention. Thinking it was some kind of animal at first, I squinted to get a better look at what exactly it was. It was about 40 yards off the left side of the tracks near a pile of rocks in an open field. At first glance, it seemed like it might be a lone cow but there were no other cows anywhere else to be seen.

I quickly pointed out this odd sight to Brad, and he attempted take a closer look while I grabbed the binoculars off the hanger. As soon as I had them up to my eyes, I could immediately see what it was that had drawn my attention. After staring at it for a few seconds, I realized that what stood before us was not an animal at all - but rather ape-like creature with long arms and legs standing upright like a human being! My jaw dropped and I handed the binoculars to Brad so he could see; his expression was one of disbelief.

As the train got closer and closer to the ape-like creature, we noticed that it didn't move a single muscle. It just stared in our direction, unblinking and seemingly unfazed by our presence. We were now close enough so that we could take in more of its features under the light of the locomotive's lamps.

The ape-like creature was around 8 feet tall with broad shoulders and long arms that hung down near its knees when standing upright. Its fur was brownish-black in color and matted together in large tufts on its head, back and legs; while the rest of its body had shorter fur from what we could see. It appeared to be quite muscular as well, with a wide chest and a thick neck that gave it an intimidating appearance.

Once we had passed the ape-like creature, Brad and I just stood there in awe of what we had seen. We exchanged glances with each other, neither of us able to find any words that properly expressed our shock. Finally, I broke through the silence and spoke in a serious tone: "Did you just see what I saw?"

Brad nodded his head slowly and replied: "Yes, yes I did."
Neither one of us could believe it - here we were, out on this
journey that was supposed to be nothing more than an
ordinary trip through Idaho…and yet here we were
witnessing something completely out of the ordinary.

I had never seen anything like it before, and my mind was
running through all the animals it had in its library but could
not match up anything to what this creature was. That's when
Brad spoke up, uttering just two words that sent a chill down
my spine: "That's Bigfoot."

I couldn't believe what I was hearing. Could it really be true?
Was the legend of Bigfoot actually true? As soon as Brad
mentioned it, my mind immediately began to match up what I
had seen on TV and the internet when there were stories of
Bigfoot sightings. It was almost like a light bulb had gone off
in my head.

The ape-like creature we saw seemed to confirm all those
reports that so many people had been making for years about
seeing this strange ape-like creature; and here we were now,
standing witness to it ourselves. The thought that something

so mysterious could be out there in plain sight made me feel both excited and scared at the same time.

As my heart began to race, I knew that this was something that we would never forget - an experience that could only be described as a true once in a lifetime moment. It was definitely clear to us that the ape-like creature we saw on the railway track was no ordinary animal. It had to be Bigfoot - the legendary ape-like creature from folklore and stories. We had finally seen it for ourselves!

Brad then asked if we should radio into our supervisor on what we had just seen. I responded in a sarcastic tone, asking him what exactly would we say? That we saw an ape-like creature standing on the railway track? It was clear that he would never believe us, and since we didn't hit it with the train there was nothing to report to management.

Brad and I made a silent agreement in that moment - this ape-like creature we saw on the railway track would forever remain between the two of us. Although a small part of me felt like what we had seen was something worth noting, I quickly weighed all of the negatives of actually speaking up about it.

The reality was that no one would ever believe us - how could they? How could anyone comprehend an ape-like creature standing right in front of them on a railway track? It seemed too wild to be true, so Brad and I decided to keep our experience to ourselves. We knew that if we spoke up and mentioned it to other people, they would just think we were crazy or making things up.

Brad and I finished our trip by Friday afternoon, just in time for me to make it home for my family's birthday party. From that day forward, whenever we worked together Brad and I would always talk about our encounter on the railway track. We were determined to find out if what we saw was real or not, so we started keeping an eye out for any ape-like creatures while we drove through the country.

Besides our newfound interest in bigfoot sightings, we also shared another passion: research. In our free time away from work, Brad and I would both independently research anything related to bigfoot sightings in the area. On our next journey together, we would discuss what each of us had learned during this research and compare our findings.

It was interesting to see how passionate Brad and I both became about the ape-like creature that we had encountered on the railway track. Although it seemed like a tall tale, we were determined to learn as much as we possibly could about it. We wanted to know what other people had experienced and if there really were more bigfoot out in the wilderness.

ENCOUNTER #15 My Dad and I See Bigfoot in Idaho

I was in my mid-thirties when I took my father on a quail hunting trip to the Clearwater region in Idaho. It had been years since we'd gone hunting together and it seemed like the perfect way to catch up and bond as my life had become busier with my own family. Besides, I knew that my dad loved to hunt, so what better way to spend time with him than doing something he enjoyed?

We planned our hunt for early fall and rented a hotel room in a small town near the public hunting land. When it was time to go, I excitedly picked up my dad in my new Chevy Silverado. After saying goodbye to mom, we loaded his things into the truck and headed out. It was a few hour drive, but the time passed quickly as we talked about what had been going on in my life and career.

When we finally arrived at the hotel, we unloaded our gear and decided to find dinner at a local restaurant. My dad loved striking up conversations with strangers and after speaking to the hotel workers and a few guests about the best places to eat in town, they directed us to a corner cafe that was known for its meat loaf dinners. Although this wasn't my favorite food, I knew it was one of my dad's favorites so I figured I could find something else to eat there.

We went inside the small diner and grabbed a booth near the window. While looking over the menu, we got into conversation with an elderly couple sitting next to us who were locals in town. They told us some stories about their life in the small town and even recommended their favorite dishes on the menu.

After we all finished our meals, my dad thanked them for the pleasant conversation before we were ready to leave. Just as we were about to go, the elderly couple mentioned something unexpected: another group of hunters had seen a ape-like creature roaming around near the public hunting land in Idaho a few days prior. They said it was around 8 feet tall with long brown hair and its face resembled a human. It sounded almost too unbelievable but curiosity got the best of me so I asked for more information about their sighting.

According to them, they had spotted this creature up in the nearby hills where hunters typically go during this time of year. Unfortunately all other details were vague or non-existent since they hadn't gotten too close to it. I thanked the couple for the story before we parted ways and my dad and I discussed what it could have been on our drive back to the hotel.

We continued to talk about the ape-like creature we had heard of throughout the night, joking if we would see it ourselves. With a newfound excitement, I made sure our gear was ready for our morning hunt before we retired to bed.

The next morning came quickly and while my dad got ready slowly as he always did, I packed all of our hunting gear into the truck. I also brought along a cooler with beverages and some sandwiches for lunch and planned that we would have dinner back in town at the same cafe after we were done hunting.

We finally set off for what promised to be an exciting day of adventure and possibility. The stories of the ape-like creature still lingered in my mind, but I quickly shifted my focus to the task at hand - hunting. After some deliberation, we decided on a spot on public land about 20 minutes out of town. We loaded our gear into the truck and drove off along the winding roads until we reached our destination.

As the sun started to crest over the horizon, a cool morning air filled with anticipation surrounded us as we stepped out of the truck. Although chilly, it was actually ideal weather for quail hunting since it takes a lot of walking and can get quite hot under normal circumstances. We grabbed our gear, double checked our supplies, and set off into the stillness of the morning.

My dad and I walked for hours but it felt like minutes as we took in all the beauty of nature around us. We spotted a few quail while out stalking but they were too far to hit with a shot - an accomplishment by itself since these birds are known for being quite evasive. After several hours, we decided to head back and enjoy some lunch at the truck before continuing our hunt in a different area.

Throughout our hunt, I couldn't help but think about the ape-like creature rumored to have been roaming around in Idaho recently. Despite not seeing anything strange or out of place during our hunt so far, I was still curious as the elderly couple at the cafe seemed convinced of the validity of the story that the other hunting party had told them.

When we arrived back at the truck, something was definitely out of order. There were large footprints leading up to my truck and what seemed to be muddy hand prints on both the front driver side window and back glass of the topper that covered my truck bed. Had someone tried breaking into my truck? With a feeling of dread, I opened the truck and noticed that everything was in order and nothing missing. Thankfully none of the windows or glass were broken which meant that whoever had been here hadn't seen anything they wanted to steal from outside so had left without taking anything.

But it still made me uneasy as I started considering if someone had come out here to steal from us. Then Dad called my attention to the muddy footprints that led up to my truck and pointed out that they didn't look like the person was wearing any shoes as you could clearly see the toes. What was even more strange, however, was their size.

The footprints were definitely larger than a human's foot with a broader heel, narrower midsection, and longer toes - almost as if they were made by an ape. They measured roughly fourteen inches long and eight inches across at their widest point which seemed too big for a human but different than what would have been left behind by a black bear or other large animal native to the area.

We stood around in stunned silence as we considered this evidence - could it be possible that a legendary ape-like creature, like the one the old couple had mentioned at the cafe, was responsible for these footprints? We started to get suspicious and wondered if someone was playing a joke on us or even if the old couple had been involved in some sick prank played on out of towners.

I told Dad that we should go try a different spot for the rest of the afternoon. It didn't feel safe leaving my truck there anymore and I was already getting nervous that someone had tampered with it. We quickly finished our sandwiches in the truck on the way to another hunting spot about fifteen minutes away.

Once there, we loaded up our guns again and headed out for our afternoon hunt; however, it was not very enjoyable for me as I kept worrying that someone had messed with my new truck. The whole time I was distracted thinking about who could have done this and if they were still nearby or had left entirely.

My mind kept wondering back to my truck, but then Dad suddenly fired a shot and dropped a quail. It was like a jolt of electricity that quickly launched me back into reality and we celebrated the first downed bird with a high five. We continued on, and within a half hour my dad had shot another one. I also got in on the action by shooting my own quail as well. Now the afternoon had really turned out to what I had been hoping it would be – a full-on hunting session with some success at the end!

The more time that passed, the less I thought about whatever had happened to my truck earlier that day. It seemed like we were having a successful hunt and I wanted to stay focused on that instead of worrying. By the time the afternoon hunt was done, we had a total of seven quail - definitely enough for us both!

The sun was starting to set and I suggested to Dad that we should probably start making our way back to the truck; he agreed, after all we were both getting hungry and he had been looking forward to ordering the meatloaf again from that cafe. We slowly started making our way back through the trails and enjoyed the beautiful cool air with our bags full of quail.

As we rounded the ridge to where my truck was parked on the other side of the field about 400 yards away, I glanced towards my truck and there I noticed something out of the ordinary again. This time it looked like a person was looking in my truck again but this time we had caught them in the act.

I stopped for a moment as I was severely upset and as I looked closer the person looking in my truck seemed very odd. Although it was getting dark, I could tell that this person must be very tall. They also appeared to be wearing very dark clothing and was wildly muscular. My heart raced and I yelled out to my dad to look over at the figure peering into my truck. He had a set of binoculars so he handed them to me, as soon as i brought the binoculars to my eyes and got them in focus for this distance I realized this was no ordinary person - it was an 8 foot tall ape-like creature covered in hair peering in my window.

I handed the binoculars to my dad and once he got a look, his eyes widened in surprise. He asked me nervously, "What should we do?" I considered yelling out but knew it wouldn't reach the ape-like creature from where we stood 400 yards away. I wished I had brought a rifle with us for this very reason – one of those could shoot at that distance, but our shotguns were only effective up to about 40 yards max. So I decided to fire off my shotgun into the air as a warning shot instead.

Sure enough, as soon as I pulled the trigger, the ape-like creature looked in our direction and then immediately ran away towards a ravine. It was incredibly fast and moved with such fluidity that it was almost like a blur. We watched as the ape-like creature disappeared into the ravine, and my dad and I stood there in shock - we had just seen Bigfoot! As we started to make our way back to my truck, I knew one thing for sure – no matter what happened next, this would be an experience I would never forget.

We got to my truck and noticed large footprints identical to the ones that we had found at our original spot. On top of that, there were now more muddy hand prints on the windows. This realization made me think back to the first parking spot. I wondered how the creature could have gotten here so quickly, but then I realized that although it was a 15 minute drive by car, if you traveled directly through terrain instead of taking winding roads, it would be much quicker. Taking into account both this fact and the four hours we had been hunting in this area already, as well as the ape-like creature's ability to move at an incredibly fast speed, this certainly was a manageable distance for it to cover in that amount of time.

My dad and I just looked at each other in disbelief, still coming to terms with what had clearly happened here. We decided it would be best to get out of this area as soon as possible so we packed up our guns and gear and headed back into town. First, we went to the hotel to drop off our gear and then decided to go back to the cafe for dinner and debrief on what exactly had happened.

We sat in the cafe chatting over dinner and trying to make sense of our experience. Dad had his usual meatloaf, while I stuck with a classic burger. As we discussed what could have been lurking in the Idaho wilderness that day, the old couple from last night walked into the diner and was seated directly behind us. They asked how our hunt went and then questioned if we had seen anything out of the ordinary. My dad looked at me with a knowing glint in his eye and said, "Oh yeah! You could say that."

We told them all about our experience seeing the ape-like creature - how we spotted it, how it moved and the footprints we found. The old couple listened to our story but almost with a sense of familiarity, as though they already knew what was living beyond the ravine. Perhaps this was why they weren't too surprised by what we told them. As they enjoyed

109

their meal, my dad and I couldn't help but feel that perhaps this wont be the last time they will hear such a tale. It seemed that these folks were well-versed in the mysteries of Idaho. After all, what else could explain their composed reaction to our story? No matter the answer, it was clear our experience with Bigfoot would not be soon forgotten.

ENCOUNTER #16 A Morning Jog With Bigfoot

It was the summer of 2018 and my newlywed wife Margaret and I had just finished renovating our home in a small town nestled between two mountain ranges in Idaho. We had known each other for over three years before we tied the knot, but it felt like only yesterday that we were standing at the altar sharing our vows. We were both older than most when we got married - I was 38 and she was 36 - but it didn't matter to us; all that mattered was that we had found love after so many years without it.

Every morning Margaret and I would take a jog through town together. It was our own little ritual, something special between us that made us feel connected as husband and wife. We'd start out early in the morning when the sun was still rising in the sky, its golden rays cascading down upon the earth like tiny fairies sprinkling dust onto a lake. As we jogged through town, we enjoyed all of the beauty around us - from tall pine trees to birds chirping in the distance - it somehow made us both feel at peace. The vast wilderness of Idaho also made us aware of just how small we were; no matter what troubles or worries weighed heavily on our minds, they seemed insignificant when compared to this great expanse of nature.

Even though we were aware of the beauty surrounding us, nothing could have prepared us for what we saw one particular morning in August. We had been out jogging as usual when something seemed to be off - an unmistakable presence lurking in the shadows that both Margaret and I felt before we actually saw it.

As we rounded a corner on the running path on the side of town, an ape-like creature stood there before us, towering over seven feet tall. Its eyes immediately turned our way in the dim morning light and its fur was a deep brown color. It literally looked like it had just been crossing the path from one side of the woods to another, seemingly unaware that anyone would even be nearby during this crossing. We stopped running immediately and just stood there, frozen in shock.

The creature was only about 30 yards away from us so we got an incredible view of its features. It had a muscular build with a wide chest and long, powerful arms that hung low by its sides. Its face was quite ape-like, with large eyes, flat nose and small ears. Its hands were huge and it's feet were thickly padded for added stability when walking. It was the most amazing thing I had ever seen - something seemingly out of this world!

Margaret and I knew at once that we had seen something extraordinary. Having both been interested in bigfoot, we instinctively recognized what it was standing before us. We often discussed the topic of bigfoot when we were working on our home renovation, and during longer road trips we would listen to bigfoot podcasts while driving together. Although both of us were believers in the creature, neither of us expected to see one up close!

We weren't sure what to do next - should we run away or just stand there? Although the creature was huge, neither of us felt any sense of intimidation from it. It seemed almost gentle in its presence and had an aura that put us at ease. But before either of us could act, the ape-like creature suddenly disappeared into the woods as quickly as it had appeared. We were left standing there in disbelief and awe. The creature moved with such grace and speed that it almost seemed to float through the air like a ghostly apparition. Its arms hung long by its sides and we could clearly see the powerful muscles through its thick fur coat. As it disappeared into the trees, so did our chance of ever seeing something like it again.

Despite the fleeting encounter, we both knew that we had witnessed something extraordinary that day. We had seen a real bigfoot in the state of Idaho and it left us with an unforgettable memory that will stay with us forever. This experience also made us realize just how small we are compared to nature's mysteries and greatness. After this morning, Margaret and I now have even more respect for animals living in the wild – from birds to bears - as well as those elusive ape-like creatures out there roaming the forests of Idaho.

From this moment on, our morning runs were even more exciting as we always hoped that we would see another one. From what we had heard on podcasts, some people who encounter bigfoot are fearful and never want to see one again. But for us, it was the complete opposite - we wanted the experience again because it was just a beautiful creature living in the wilderness. This experience has fueled our love for this mysterious ape-like creature, and motivated us to take action in protecting its habitat and preserving its legacy in Idaho.

We now have an incredible appreciation for these creatures and their place in nature's grand plan. We understand that they may remain elusive to most of humanity but know how important they are to the environment and community. We take comfort in knowing that they still exist and remain a part of our world. This is why we continue to share our story of the bigfoot sighting in Idaho and encourage others to protect this mysterious creature. Whether it's through podcasts, books or simply spreading awareness about the importance of conservation, we will always do what we can to keep these ape-like creatures alive in our hearts and minds.

It has been an incredible journey for Margaret and I since that fateful day. Our experience with the bigfoot has taught us many things about life, nature, and ourselves - but most importantly it has reminded us just how important it is to be open-minded and accept that nothing is certain until you see it with your own eyes. We hope that our story can inspire others to embark on their own journey of discovery and witness the majestic beauty of bigfoot in its natural habitat.

ENCOUNTER #17 Fence Builder Encounters a Bigfoot

It was a crisp Saturday afternoon in the small community of Idaho Falls, Idaho. The year was 2020 and I, Jackson, had been working in construction for years. With my extra time on the weekends, I decided to take up fence building for cash as an additional source of income to help cover bills.

This particular day I had two friends helping me - Alex and David - both were happy to be taking part in something that would benefit our families with extra cash while also getting some fresh air at the same time. We worked diligently throughout the morning under the overcast sky until noon when we finally decided to take a much deserved break.

We all shared our plans for the rest of the weekend. Alex mentioned how he had been looking forward to going on a fishing trip with his family, while David talked about how he had been saving up to get himself a new gaming system - I teased him as he was much younger than me and I could not spend money on something like that as I had a family to support.

As for me, I shared that I had been busy getting my house ready for the upcoming holiday season and decorating it with festive ornaments. We were so caught up in our conversations that we were not paying much attention to what was going on around us.

We were so caught up in our conversations that we barely noticed the rustling from the nearby woods. Suddenly, I saw a flash of movement but could not make out what it was. Knowing that I was the oldest and most curious of the group, I told my friends to stay back while I went out to investigate. At first, I had wondered if an elk had made its way into town since there were developments on the other side of the road.

I cautiously crossed the street and stepped into the woods. I had no idea what I was about to discover, but something inside me told me it would be worth investigating. The trees swayed in the wind and leaves shifted across my path - nothing seemed amiss - yet I still felt like there was something out there. After walking for a few minutes, all I could see were trees swaying in the wind and leaves shifting across my path - nothing else seemed amiss so I decided to turn back and finish my lunch with Alex and David.

It was when I returned to my friends that they asked if I had seen anything, and I told them no - that it was just the wind. We finished up our lunch and got back to work; we had all hoped to finish up the fence in the next few hours so that we could all enjoy those weekend plans we had. The afternoon work went smoothly and we joked with each other all afternoon, until it was around 3:45 when I went back to the truck to grab some more nails.

That's when I looked back into the woods where I had seen movement earlier in the day. This time, I noticed something again - it almost seemed like there was a person over there looking at me. At first, I wondered if it was a neighborhood kid, but it seemed oddly large - the figure was behind much brush and trees so it was not really visible. Then, it seemed to go further back into the woods.

My curiosity got the best of me, so I crossed the road and went to get a better look. But when I got there, I could no longer see anything - whatever had been looking at me seemed to be gone. Feeling uneasy as if I was being watched, I turned around to head back to the guys. That's when I heard a branch crack behind me and quickly spun around. In just a fleeting glance, I saw the head of a creature behind some brush about 40 yards away. It was just a brief glimpse but it was very high in the air and it looked ape-like with fur covering its head. Again, the sighting was so brief and then it went crashing further into the woods; I could hear it for some time but no longer saw it.

I walked deep into the woods towards where I had seen the ape-like creature, and noticed its path leading away. For me to have been able to see its head it must have been nearly 8 feet tall - surely this was no neighborhood kid. But it was long gone so I decided to head back to my friends.

On my walk back across the street, I was trying to figure out what had just happened as well as what I should tell them. When I finally got to the backyard they asked me in a joking tone what took me so long; it took me a moment to answer and then I said that I had gone back across the road. They asked why, and I told them about how I saw something out there again and that I went to investigate.

As I was telling my friends about the ape-like creature I had seen, they asked if I was serious and I said yes. Across the street, I had just seen a creature with ape-like features! They were skeptical but eventually, from my expression and tone, they believed me. Well, I'm not sure if they believed that I saw something like Bigfoot or if they simply believed that I did see something but that I had misidentified a different animal.

We all still wanted to finish up the job quickly, so we continued on with our work. We were able to complete the fence in the next hour and as we packed up the truck and drove out of the neighborhood. I kept an eye on the woods but did not see anything out of the ordinary, though I knew that I had experienced something strange that afternoon even though my friends were still skeptical.

It was a mystery that I still could not solve; I still think about this experience often and wish that I would have got a better look at the figure. Though it was only a brief glimpse, what I saw seemed ape-like with fur covering its head - leading me to believe it may have been Bigfoot. Still, with the sighting being so quick there is no way I can say for sure that it was a bigfoot.

ENCOUNTER #18 A Girl's Chilling Encounter with Bigfoot

I was fifteen years old when I saw a Bigfoot. It was the summer, and I had been dating my boyfriend for about six months. We went to the same school, and he was my first boyfriend. He lived about two miles away from where I lived; usually, we would see each other at school and had only been to the movies a couple of times together.

This particular weekend, however, my parents were out of town and I decided to take matters into my own hands. Without telling anyone, I devised a plan that would allow me to drive myself over there on our four-wheeler instead of asking someone else for a ride. The plan involved taking side streets and crossing a field on the edge of town to get to his place, with the aim of visiting him for an hour or two.

My parents had always warned me against taking the four-wheeler on public roads and always letting them know when I was going out. I knew they would not approve of this plan, but my adolescent mind convinced me that it wouldn't hurt if I just did it this one time. So, that's what I set out to do.

Little did I know that my decision to visit my boyfriend without permission would result in something far greater than a simple visit. It was about 10 am when I decided to take the four-wheeler and headed out. Once I got on the four-wheeler, I felt a sudden rush of nervousness coursing through me, knowing that if my parents found out they would definitely not be happy with me.

Nevertheless, I texted Justin and he confirmed his parents had gone shopping for a few hours - the perfect opportunity for an undiscovered visit. My nervousness slowly turned into excitement as I sped down side roads and eventually made it to the field which was private property but well known by many people who drove ATVs to cut through this side of town instead of going into the busy streets in town.

I was speeding through the field, trying to get out of there as quickly as I could. The trail cut through an open area but curved into a wooded area about halfway through. It was well-worn from many ATVs that used it regularly, and I was going faster than I should have been. Suddenly, my eyes caught a glimpse something on the left side of the path in a small clearing. My first thought was that it must be the landowner and he had seen me speeding by. But as I got closer, I realized this wasn't a human - at least not fully human. It looked ape-like, with long arms and fur covering its body.

My heart instantly started pounding as I continued by. The creature was tall and had human expression, with a large head, long arms, and fur covering its body. Its face was mostly hidden in the shadows but it seemed to be watching me intently as I passed by. It also took a step towards the path, which only increased my anxiety and sent my heart racing even faster. Knowing that it wasn't safe for me to linger any longer, I decided to hit the throttle hard and get out of there as fast as possible.

I was in shock as my mind raced to process what I had just seen. After a few moments of terror, I finally focused all my attention on the path ahead of me and sped away from the ape-like figure standing on the path behind me. As I glanced back at him one last time before leaving the clearing, I realized that the figure was still watching me as I sped away. A chill ran down my spine and I knew to not stop until I had reached Justin's place.

In just a few more minutes, I managed to get there and parked the four-wheeler in his driveway. Justin was waiting for me sitting on his front steps when he saw me arrive and walked up to me with excitement. But as I took off my helmet, he could instantly tell something was wrong. He asked me what was going on and I told him that I wanted to go inside and would tell him then.

We went inside and down to his bedroom, where I immediately broke down into tears. Justin was shocked but stayed by my side as he comforted me until my tears stopped flowing. After a few moments, he asked me what had happened and why I was so upset.

I took a deep breath before telling him that I had just seen something very strange in the woods. His eyes widened with disbelief, but he stayed calm and let me tell him everything in detail. I described how I was driving on a private field when suddenly I saw ape-like creature standing on the left side of the path in a small clearing. It was tall and ape-like, with a large head, long arms, and fur covering its body. Its face was mostly hidden in the shadows, but it seemed to be watching me as I passed by. It even took a step towards the path, which only increased my anxiety.

I finished my recount of events and Justin just looked at me in astonishment. After a few moments, he told me that he had heard stories of bigfoot on some of the shows he watched and he said that it sounded like a bigfoot. I nodded in agreement, feeling both relieved and amazed for having seen such an amazing creature with my own eyes. We talked about this mysterious ape-like creature for several more minutes and then he asked me if I wanted a glass of water.

When Justin was gone from his room for only a few minutes, my mind started racing as I realized that going through the woods to get home was the best way to go undetected on the four-wheeler. Knowing this meant I would have a difficult decision to make. Should I take the same trail back home and risk seeing the bigfoot again, or take the safer option of driving through town and risk being seen by the police? These thoughts weighed heavily on my mind as I finished my glass of water.

We hung out for another hour before it was time to go, as his parents would likely be getting home soon. As we walked outside, Justin asked if we should just tell his parents so they could give me a ride home and we could get the four-wheeler later; he had a worried look on his face. Despite my fear of getting caught, I turned down his offer and decided to risk driving back through busier streets to get home rather than going back through the woods.

Luck was with me and my drive home was uneventful; I made it back without being detected by anyone. I pulled the four-wheeler into the garage and shut the garage door, making sure all doors were locked. It was frightening to me knowing that a bigfoot was out there just a mile or so away from my house.

I spent the afternoon and night at home alone, as my parents would not return home until tomorrow. I called Justin several times throughout the day and night to help keep me occupied and comforted. We talked about what had happened earlier in the day and tried to make sense of it all, but neither of us could come up with any answers. The only thing we knew for certain was that Bigfoot exists! This is something that many people still don't believe, but I know it's true because I saw it with my own eyes. It was an experience I will never forget!

ENCOUNTER #19 The Cover Up of a Bigfoot Sighting

It was June of 2015 and I had just completed my finance degree from the University of Idaho. With a new job as a credit analyst starting in two weeks, I decided to maximize my free time by exploring this beautiful state that I called home. My best friend from college, Amber, had also recently finished her undergrad studies and agreed to join me for this adventure. We considered going on a hike but instead opted for an easy walk along the Snake River at the Perrine Memorial Bridge in Twin Falls, Idaho.

Amber and I had been friends since freshman year of college. We both shared a love for learning, outdoor activities, and having a good time. In our four years together, we created an unbreakable bond that made us believe we would be lifelong friends. After graduating, we moved out of the dorms and decided to rent an apartment together; it was the perfect way to stay connected while also starting our new lives as adults. We spent many nights laughing over wine while planning future adventures in the great outdoors - this hike along the Snake River was no exception.

We arrived at the bridge around noon on a sunny day with clear blue skies above us. The view of the river was breathtaking as it snaked its way through all kinds of terrain before eventually reaching our destination. The bridge itself is quite majestic – spanning 440 feet across the river and standing nearly 200 feet above it – yet we felt so small standing below it. As we began to walk along the trail, we easily kept our conversation going, as we always did, about things going on in our lives. I described to Amber how I was nervous and excited about starting my new job and she told me about the several interviews she had over the last two weeks and which ones she was most excited about getting a potential offer from.

After about an hour of walking along the trail, we decided to take a break near the river. We sat down at a nearby rock and enjoyed a snack while admiring the beautiful landscape around us. It was incredibly peaceful; all that could be heard were the birds singing in the trees and the occasional fish jumping from the water below. As we soaked in our surroundings, I saw something on the other side of the river out of my peripheral vision.

I stared at the figure for a few seconds before comprehending what I was seeing. I was confused, and told Amber to take a look. After a brief moment, it went behind a stack of rocks and we didn't see it again. We were both perplexed as to what it could have been, so we finished our snack and continued our walk.

About 10 minutes later, when we were parallel to where the creature had originally been on the other side of the river, we saw it again – creature with a dark coat of fur standing still and looking directly at us from across the river. We were completely dumbfounded, unable to comprehend what we were seeing after all this time.

After about 10 seconds, it quickly jumped into some nearby bushes and vanished. We stared in awe for several minutes before finally realizing that could have been a Bigfoot! It was incredible; there was no denying it was ape-like, had a thick furry coat, and stood upright just like any other human. From beginning to end, the encounter lasted less than two minutes – but it felt like an eternity.

I couldn't believe what we had witnessed and was relieved when Amber said she saw it too - if only one of us had seen it, I'm sure we would have written off the experience as our imaginations running wild. We weren't sure if we should report this to someone but who would we even report this sighting to? The police? Amber thought we should because she said that if it ended up hurting someone, she would feel terrible that we didn't say anything, but I wasn't so sure they would even believe us.

Regardless, Amber made a call to 911 and told the operator what we saw - a huge ape-like creature at least eight feet tall and several hundred pounds. The operator asked if she was sure or if perhaps we had mistaken a bear or something for what we saw. We were adamant about what we had seen, and

Amber eventually convinced the operator to send an officer out to investigate.

As we made our way back to the apartment, Amber seemed more fearful than I was. She asked if I thought the police would actually investigate, or if they were just telling us that to make us feel better. I told her I wasn't sure but that if they truly found something there were probably two options of what could happen - either it would be reported and all over the news, or they would cover up the occurrence in order to not scare away tourists who come for the trails.

We were left in limbo following the encounter, with nothing to do but wonder what would come of it. We waited several days for news about what had happened but nothing came out. We assumed that this meant the police had decided to cover up whatever it was that we saw or they never found anything.

While it felt strange knowing that an ape-like creature could be out there and the public was not aware of it, we discussed doing something more to make people aware about this possibility over the next few days. However, life quickly got busy with both Amber receiving a job offer from the top company she wanted to work for and me starting my new job as well. With our lives preoccupied, we ultimately never got around to taking any further action.

This experience was one of the most incredible ones we've ever had and it's not something we forget easily. We often wonder what life might be like if everyone knew about these ape-like creatures that exist in Idaho. Our state is home to a vast array of wildlife, but perhaps Bigfoot remains the biggest mystery of them all.

Whatever happened that day still remains unknown to us, but as more people recount their own stories, maybe someday soon enough someone will solve this mysterious creature that exists in our state. Until then, however, its existence will remain only whispers amongst those who have been lucky enough to encounter it.

ENCOUNTER #20 The Town Drunk's Encounter with Bigfoot

I first caught sight of the creature at the end of summer, in the year 2002. I had been living in my trailer home and working as a welder around town for years, ever since my parents bought me the land and and trailer home when I turned 21. Though some people considered me to be a bit off, I enjoyed my life out in the country, free from any distractions and often alone, some even thought i was a drunk but although I had a few drinks here and there it was never to the level that was rumored, it was a 20 acre plot that I had and was mostly covered in trees and brush but around me were corn fields, it was like my property was a postage stamp of woods with open fields around me, the 10 acres that were field I had been renting to a farmer that lived nearby and although it was not alot of money for renting I had nothing better to do with the field.

It was the early morning of a Tuesday, before the sun began to rise, that I first noticed something strange near my property. I had stepped outside with my dog in tow to take him for a quick walk before heading off to work when suddenly I saw a shadow move quickly across the short dirt driveway that connected my property to the county highway leading into town.

With the light still being dim at this hour, it was hard for me make out exactly what it was, yet it appeared very tall and walked quite like a human being. As soon as it saw me, however, it quickly darted away and disappeared within seconds amongst the trees. Though there were plenty of wild animals living in the countryside around me, something about the way it moved left me feeling perplexed.

Having to get to work soon, I decided against exploring this further and continued on my way. Nevertheless, I thought over what had just happened during my drive and came to the conclusion that I must have mistaken what I saw as I was still groggy at that time from having just waken up; who or what could have been so tall and agile enough to move as quickly as it did? These questions flooded my mind as I made my way into town, yet they would remain unanswered until later.

When I got off work, I had nearly forgotten about the experience but after pulling into my driveway, I remembered the shadow so decided to park my car and walk back onto the dirt driveway. To my surprise, there in plain sight were two large footprints, both only partially visible due to the fact that I had driven over them twice - once on my way to work and once as I arrived home. Despite the partial visibility of these tracks, I could still make out that they were much larger than any creature I was aware of.

I was filled with a sense of awe as I examined the footprints. It was clear to me that whatever had made them was not a normal animal, for their shape and size were unlike anything I had seen before. Baffled by this discovery, I followed the prints across the driveway and into the small woods that surrounded my house but I only saw one more possible indentation on the grass until they suddenly stopped altogether. My heart thumped wildly in my chest as I tried to comprehend what could have made these large footprints. Despite my curiosity, all I could do is wonder about my strange sighting so I went back inside and relaxed for an hour or so before making myself a frozen pizza for dinner and watching some TV, I also had a few beers.

Around 9pm, I decided to go outside for a smoke and to let my dog out one last time for the night. As I stood there enjoying the crisp summer night air, I heard an amazing howl coming from the neighboring farms woods that were on the other side of the open fields surrounding my property. It was such a long and drawn out howl that seemed to last almost 30 seconds in one single breath - something only an incredibly large creature could have been able to produce. After I finished my cigarette and called my pup back inside, I went back into bed thinking about the strange events of the day and all of its mysteries yet unsolved.

When I woke the next morning, I did my usual routine of letting my dog out before heading to work. This time, instead of seeing a shadow cross my driveway as I had done the previous day, I noticed something else unusual - large footprints that went past my car and around the back side of my house. Immediately concerned, I stepped down from my steps to get a better look at these prints. They seemed to be made by the same creature that had left its tracks in my driveway just 24 hours earlier; however, these tracks were even closer than before! Not only did this mean that some mysterious creature was roaming around but it also meant that whatever it was had been within 10 feet of where I slept. I was filled with a sense of dread and wonder.

Although my sense of safety had been shaken, I knew I had to get to work. As I drove, the questions surrounding whatever creature had been lurking around my house lingered in my mind. After a long day at work, I headed home and wondered if anything else had happened while I was gone - but when I arrived there were only the same footprints by my car from that morning. I quickly went inside and loaded my shotgun before placing it beside the front door; this way if anyone or anything attempted to break in, I would be prepared with a weapon. That night, after making myself some dinner in the microwave, I stepped outside for one last smoke and let out the dog - and again heard that mysterious howl echoing from the distance.

I continued to stand outside for a few more moments, still captivated by the mysteries of the last two days, before I finally went back inside and prepared myself for sleep. As I lay in my bed that night, I wondered what kind of creature could be roaming around my small town in Idaho - and why it had chosen to visit me. These questions left me feeling uneasy as I drifted off into a deep slumber.

I woke up the next morning on Friday, with an even greater curiosity than before. What had happened overnight around my property? I quickly got out of bed and went outside to let my dog out before heading off to work. To my relief, nothing unusual had occurred; however, I still couldn't help but wonder what was lurking in the shadows.

The day at work dragged on as I was physically exhausted from lack of sleep and the stress of the last two days. I was, however, excited for the day to end as it was payday. After work I treated myself to dinner at a local restaurant that also had a bar. I enjoyed broasted chicken and talked with regulars for several hours - and maybe had one too many drinks! It was around 11 pm when I finally left the bar and began my five-mile drive home. All along the journey back I felt nervous; not because of any sightings on my property, but because if a cop pulled me over I would be arrested for drunk driving. When I finally made the turn into my dirt driveway, I let out a sigh of relief knowing that I had made it home without incident.

As I continued down my dirt driveway I felt a sense of safety return; almost as if the events of the last few days had never happened. I had allowed myself to drink more than usual, perhaps as a way to forget about whatever mysterious creature was lurking around my property. As I approached my house however, something caught my eye - and when I stopped the car and looked closer, there it was - an ape-like creature with grey fur that seemed to shimmer in the night light.

It stood close to 7 feet tall and its weight was likely around 300 pounds. Its head was large with small black eyes and ape like ears, while its muscular arms hung below their shoulders. It held itself upright like a human but lacked any clothing or accessories. Its face was emotionless and it seemed to be peering into my kitchen window. I could feel the fear start to rise in my chest as I stared back at this foreign creature, unsure of what to do next.

I felt my heart stop as I watched the ape-like creature turn its head from peering into my kitchen window to look directly at me. Its face was illuminated by the headlights of my car and I could see it clearly for the first time - it was unbelievably human-like. All I could think about was Harry and the Hendersons, a movie about a family who discovers an ape-like creature. Was this really Bigfoot?

I sat there in disbelief, my eyes still glued to the ape-like creature that had appeared out of the night. It seemed completely unfazed by me, like it knew that I could do nothing to hurt it due to its incredible size difference. I was unsure what to do as I did not have a way to turn around in my driveway. I considered backing out and leaving, but after just a moment the creature turned around and walked towards the back of my house before disappearing into the darkness of the small woods that surrounded my property.

In shock, I sat there for a few minutes longer before finally pulling my car into its parking spot and quickly making my way inside, locking the doors behind me. My heart was pounding as I tried to process what had just happened - could all of those tales about Bigfoot actually be true? I sat there for a bit longer before finally going to bed. I was pretty drunk so even though I had just witnessed something incredible I was able to fall asleep relatively quickly.

The next morning, I woke up much later than usual; my hangover was the culprit. I made myself a pot of coffee and prepared to head outside to let the dog out for its morning stroll. Then, like a bolt of lightning, it hit me - the creature from last night had been real! In my drunken haze I hadn't been sure if all I had seen had really happened or not. Had I actually witnessed a Bigfoot?

I stepped out into the crisp morning air and let the dog run off around the yard. As my gaze drifted towards where I had seen it the night before, something caught my eye- fresh footprints in the dirt! My heart skipped a beat as I realized that what I saw couldn't have been a figment of my imagination - it had really happened. I shook my head in disbelief at the thought; was this really proof of Bigfoot? Either way, one thing was for certain - whatever it was, it had been real.

That day I lazed around my house with a few naps trying to work off the hangover and mostly just lounging, but every little bit of time I again thought about the creature and wondered if it was still somewhere nearby. When night approached, I did my usual routine to let the dog out one last time and to have a smoke before bed; however, tonight I did not hear the howls in the distance nor was there anything out of the ordinary on my property.

I remained vigilant for several weeks afterward but never saw or heard anything more from the creature. I believe that whatever it was curious about on my property must have decided to move on. For a long time I wondered if I should tell anyone about my experience, and ultimately I decided it would be best not to; anyone who saw me at the bar that night knew how much I had to drink so they would probably have said that it was the alcohol that caused me to see things. But to this day, I will stand by the fact that I saw a Bigfoot on my property that night.

The stories of Bigfoot in Idaho have been around for decades, and now, I can say that I am a witness to one myself. Seeing those tracks the next day was enough proof for me – something ape-like had come onto my property and made its presence known. Whether or not it was actually Bigfoot is up to speculation, but I will always remember that night as if it were yesterday.

Conclusion

The stories in this book provide compelling evidence that Bigfoot exists in Idaho and beyond. From the tales of ape-like creatures seen by individuals while hiking, to a Girl's eye-witness account of a Bigfoot sighting on a four-wheeler, there is ample proof that these mysterious ape-like creatures exist and roam the roads and trails of our state.

These experiences are not isolated cases but rather part of a larger body of evidence which suggests that Bigfoot is more than just an urban legend. With each new tale we hear, the reality of these ape-like beings draws closer and closer to us; it may be only a matter of time before we find them living among us.

Yet even as we wait for our first undeniable photo or video of a Bigfoot, we can take solace in knowing that these mysterious ape-like creatures are out there. Their presence adds an element of mystery and intrigue to the outdoors; this is why so many people choose to go on their own searches for Bigfoot.

We may never know the full extent of what lies beyond our vision, but it doesn't mean that we can't keep looking. The stories contained in this book prove that if you look closely enough, you just might find your own evidence of the existence of Bigfoot.

Who knows? With a little bit of luck and determination, perhaps you too will get to experience the thrill of a lifetime like those featured here did! Go ahead and take the search for Bigfoot into your own hands and find out for yourself what mysteries may be lurking in the woods.

Printed in Great Britain
by Amazon

20941425R00081